DEEP-FRIED SWEETHEARTS
Holidays in Lake Point 2

Sarah Cass

Sensual Romance

Mainstream Romance

Sarah Cass

www.authorsarahcass.com

Divine Roses Ink Publishing

www.divinerosesink.com

A Divine Roses Ink Book
Mainstream Romance
Sensual Romance
Deep-Fried Sweethearts
Copyright © 2014 Sarah Cass
Second E-book Publication: September 2015
First E-book Publication: January 2014

Cover design by Sarah Cass
Edited by Megan Koenen
Proofread by M.S. Daniels
All cover art and logo copyright © 2013 by Sarah Cass

PUBLISHER
Divine Roses Ink
http://www.divinerosesink.com

Books by Sarah Cass

The Tribe Series

The Tribe

The Wolf

The Chief

The Raven

The Dominion Falls Series

Changing Tracks

Derailed

Dark Territory

Runaway Train

Home Signal

The Lake Point Series

Santa, Maybe

Deep-Fried Sweethearts

Stalled Independence

Witch Way

A Thorough Thanksgiving

Eve's New Year

Heartstrings & Hockey Pucks

Luck of the Cowgirl

Stars, Stripes & Motorbikes

Free Falling

Love for Hire

Stand Alone Novels

Masked Hearts

Leap

Dedication

To my husband.
One year later and you're still supporting my dream.
Thank you.

Chapter One

Michaela bent down to pull open the bottom drawer of the file cabinet. As had been her luck every other time she tried to open it in the past few weeks, the damn thing stuck. She jerked once, twice, and on the third time the drawer opened fast enough to almost make her fall flat on her ass.

A light tap hit her doorframe just before the voice she'd grown to loathe years ago.

"Still the best damn view in town. Think it's gotten better, even. You're getting some curves, Mikey."

As was a customary response to said voice, a strange feeling crept up her spine until her nose wrinkled.

"Shut up, Gary." She gathered up the game schedules for The Midway, her fair-themed restaurants, carnival games she'd been after and straightened. When she turned, she kicked the drawer shut. "What the hell are you doing in Lake Point?"

"Um, it was just Christmas. What do you think I'm doing here?"

"Trying to con your parents out of some more money in the name of the holiday?"

He slipped from the doorway into the office without asking permission. While she walked over to the desk he had the gall to peer at the papers on her desk. "Don't be silly. I'm just visiting. Thought I'd stay a while."

At her desk, Michaela slammed her game schedules down on top of the financial papers he'd been leering at. "Cal will be happy to have something to do, arresting you soon as he gets a chance."

"Aw, come on Mikey. Don't be like that." Gary turned on his charming smile with alarming speed. If she hadn't grown immune the day she'd realized his many crimes, both personal and legal, she might have been worried about falling for his false charms once again. "I thought you'd be happy to see me."

"You thought wrong. I was *happy* when you left town with your latest flavor of the month three years ago." She leaned on the desk. "We're divorced. You're not welcome in my home or my business."

"Public place, baby. I can come and go as I want."

"The restaurant, yes. Not my office. Get out." She pointed to the door to emphasize, but he only smirked. "Don't make me call Cal," she said as a final threat.

He heaved a dramatic sigh. "You don't have to be like that. I'll go. Just wanted to talk."

"I'm not interested in talking. It's over, and been over for a long time. Just leave me alone." She dropped into her chair. Rather than give him the satisfaction of replying to his continued griping over her attitude, she turned her attention to the schedule.

Almost five minutes passed before she no longer heard him, and just the regular sounds of the shop reached her ear. A look up from her papers to the door proved he was long gone. She sighed and sank back in her chair.

The Midway's short year of business had made it famous for her variety of candy and fair-style food available all year long. Her insanely busy Christmas season, filled with cookies, candies, special holiday-themed carnival games, and decorations, had immediately been replaced by the chaos of the upcoming Valentine's Day holiday.

This year in addition to her responsibilities to the business, and creating a brand new specialty candy for the holiday, she'd made the insane choice of helping to plan the town's newest community party. Like Christmas on the Square, Sweethearts On The Square promised to be bigger, and wrap up with a romantic dance for the adults.

As tired and stressed as she was, the last thing she needed was her ex hanging around again. Between his cheating, lying, and drug abuse, she was more than glad to be rid of him. If only he'd stayed gone, life might be perfect.

The pop of a balloon followed by cheers replaced the smile she'd lost with Gary's arrival. Someone just won the balloon and dart game. The first since she'd put it up last week. Surprisingly enough, the dart game proved to be far more popular than the fish bowl game it had replaced.

Of course, the permanent skee ball game won out every month for popularity. She'd never meant to keep any game permanent, but rather rotate them monthly, but skee ball proved too popular to get rid of. If she had the room, she'd install a second one.

Another knock disrupted her train of thought. A familiar, "Excuse me, Miss O'Keefe?" came from the doorway. Of course, if her business thoughts had to be disrupted there could be no better way than with Owen Montague, better known simply as Tag. Ten years her junior, he'd grown up into quite a looker.

She could remember joking with her friend, Eve, five

years ago about Tag being jail bait for women like them. Now he was lethally legal at the age of twenty-one, and even better looking with azure eyes, mussed blond hair, and a crooked smile that she bet had melted the panties off of many girls in his class. Just when she realized she'd been staring at him and jolted out of her reverie, he rewarded her with that signature grin, and she swore her heart skipped a beat. She shook her head to clear it.

"Yes, Tag?"

"I saw your ad. Jake suggested I apply; I've been looking for something permanent instead of odd jobs." Tag crossed the room and held out some paperwork. "Application, resume, and a few letters of recommendation."

"You want the assistant manager position?" Try though she might, Michaela couldn't keep the doubt from her voice. She flipped through the papers.

"Yes. I finished getting my Bachelor's degree back in December, so I need something full time. Floating odd jobs isn't bad, but I'd like something permanent." He leaned on the desk, and her gaze immediately flew to the flex of muscle in his forearms. "I hope you'll at least look at my resume. You might be surprised."

"Letters from Jake and Eve both?" She pursed her lips. Jake owned the antique shop in town, Past Over, Eve was his manager, and her good friend. "Overkill, don't you think?"

"Can't ever have too many letters of recommendation. Miss Ellery insisted."

She knew if she looked up that damn grin would do her in, so she kept her focus on the papers before her. After she'd flipped through the stack of letters, she set it on the desk. "I'll look this over and we'll meet on Monday for a proper interview. I'll allow you that."

"Thanks, Miss O'Keefe. You won't regret it." He held out his hand. When she responded with her own, his warm hand folded hers in a gentle, but firm handshake.

"Easy, Tag. I haven't given you the job yet." She could swear the heat of his hand travelled up to flood her cheeks. If she did give him the job, working alongside such eye candy would be rough—especially with how easily she blushed.

"I know. Let's just say I've got a good feeling."

So do I. Oops, hush your inner voice. She had no doubt she was blushing now, but forced herself to smile and nod. "We'll see if it stays. Monday at nine work for you for an interview? I'd like to get it over with before I open for the day."

"Nine sharp. Thanks." He released her hand and ran his hand through his tousled locks. The kid knew he had it going on. Damn him. "See you then."

"See you then." Michaela stood until Tag left the room, and proceeded to drop into her chair with a groan. "I'm beyond screwed, and I'm going to kill Eve if she sent him here," she muttered to herself.

It would be tough to turn him down, and not just for his looks. Her quick perusal of his resume had impressed her. A Bachelor's degree in business beat out the lack of a true steady job for several years.

The stack of recommendation letters from half the business owners in town worked against her resolve to not hire someone so young. Not age discrimination, but experience.

After her divorce and the hellish two years after, the idea for the business had pulled her out of the pit of depression. She'd worked hard for two long years to get the plan in place and the financing. Every bit of her heart and soul had been poured into creating The Midway. The hard work had paid off, and everyone young and old liked her restaurant, even without a liquor license.

She wasn't sure if she should risk everything on an inexperienced young man.

Unfortunately, she couldn't go on like she was, either. The Midway had grown into a successful business in the past year, but she pulled one-hundred-twenty hour weeks to keep it viable.

She needed the help badly. Like, yesterday.

Right then her best option was Tag. Young, inexperienced Tag. The rest of her staff consisted of high school or college students, or grandmothers that couldn't, or wouldn't, take on the full time plus overtime work week an assistant manager position would mean.

The ad she'd placed in her desperation had garnered very few worthwhile candidates.

Then along came Tag.

She wondered if there was a pill that would control blushing. One double-entendre and she'd be done for.

* * * *

The Diner was almost empty of customers by the time Tag got there. Inside a woman wiped down the counter, her graying blond hair edging out of the bun she always put it in to start her day. Short and slim, she still looked young despite years of hard work. His aunt had worked almost every day of his life, even as she'd raised him while first serving at, and then owning The Diner.

He entered with a sheepish duck of his head. "Hey, Aunt Myrtle."

"Tag, my boy." She set down her rag and grabbed a glass. "Your usual?"

"I can get it myself Auntie-M." He teased as he took the glass and went to the pop machine. "Busy today?"

"Blessedly so, son. We were packed most of the afternoon. Surprised you didn't see from where you were." Myrtle nodded toward the front windows where there was a clear view of the auto shop across the street. "Any luck rebuilding that hunk of junk?"

"Not much." Tag swirled his drink around in its glass and frowned. "I couldn't seem to focus today. I think I just got in Clay's way. He gave up at around three and went to work on paying repairs. Not that I blame him, that old Nova might be beyond hope."

"Why do you want to rebuild it anyhow? It's been sitting around my barn for years."

The Nova was the last, and only, thing he remembered about his parents. He could still hear his mom teasing his dad about the "no-go" car. When he was four he didn't understand, but he did now. He sighed and set down his glass. "I just needed a project, I guess."

She patted his hand, and then resumed wiping the counter. "That's more than a project, it's a life sentence. It's your money and time, though. I can't fault you there."

He cleared his throat and downed his drink. As he refilled it, he said over his shoulder, "I turned in my resume at The Midway today."

"Good boy. What did Mikey have to say?"

"Ugh. I hate that nickname." He wrinkled his nose and sat at the counter. "She looks nothing like someone named Mikey. She's sure not a tomboy; she's all elegant and womanly."

"That so?" Her brow arched and her lips twitched. "Are you crushing on an older woman?"

Truthfully he'd had a crush on her for years. Since his babysitter, Wendy, had brought Michaela over to do homework one night he'd liked the redhead. He'd not yet hit puberty, but he still thought she was pretty. His thoughts hadn't changed all these years later. "I'm trying to get her to hire me, not date me." Not yet, anyway.

"So you are still crushing on Mikey O'Keefe? I thought you'd stopped that years ago." She chuckled and shook her head. "Boy, you are in for a heap of trouble if you work there. Are you sure it's smart?"

"Well, you won't hire me."

"No sir. You're making your own way just fine. I intend to keep it that way."

"I can't keep doing the odd jobs, and I know I can do the job she needs me to do." He twirled his glass in the condensation circle it had created on the counter. If he met his aunt's eyes now he'd be caught. He did like Michaela, had for years, but he also really wanted this job. "I've wanted to work at The Midway since day one. I thought I could bring in Grandma's candy recipes, but she wasn't looking for anything but part time help, and I had enough part time gigs."

"Defensive." She leaned on the counter across from him. "All right, mister. I'll leave you be, but you still haven't told me what she said."

"She agreed to an interview, but she didn't sound very positive."

"You'll just charm her like you always do."

Tag wrinkled his nose when she tapped it with her finger. "I'd rather get hired because I can do the job, not because I can charm someone." Although he didn't imagine with Michaela it would take much. He could still picture her deep red blush that had so easily filled her cheeks and seeped down her elegant neck.

His aunt was right; he was in a heap of trouble.

The doors to the kitchen swung open with a bang when Myrtle walked back into the kitchen. "Just remember to dress right and shave that scruff off your face," she yelled over her shoulder.

"I like my scruff."

"Fine, be a ragamuffin," she hollered from the back.

He laughed and finished off his drink. After a moment he brushed his fingers along his chin and wondered if Michaela liked the scruff. "Yeah. I'm in a heap of trouble."

* * * *

Tag shook the snow off his coat outside the door before hanging it on a hook. For what might have been the hundredth time that day he adjusted his collar, buttoned his top button again, and immediately unbuttoned it.

Once he'd exhaled his frustration, he ran his fingers through his hair and walked back toward the office. One of the women in the kitchen called to him and waved her fingers. Tracy, two years his junior. She'd always made her affections for him clear. He'd never cared for dating anyone younger than him, though.

Even in high school he'd never dated anyone younger. All of his girlfriends had been at least the same grade, if not older, than he was.

Out of politeness, he returned her wave before heading down the short hall to the office. Inside Michaela chewed on the end of a pen, her red hair curtained around her face in loose curls. Only good manners kept him from staring for as long as he wanted to.

He knocked on the doorframe. "Miss O'Keefe, are you ready for me? I know I'm a little early."

She released the death grip her teeth had on the pen and lifted her head in surprise. Her stunning blue eyes focused on him before she dropped the pen all together. "Oh. Tag. I'm sorry, I was distracted and didn't realize it was already almost nine. Please, come in."

While she shuffled papers around and added to the haphazard stack beside her, he took the seat across the desk from her. "Thank you again for agreeing to the interview."

"Of course. With so many letters of reference, I'd have to be a fool not to, right?" She offered a smile before she turned around to grab an envelope from the table behind her desk. "Here we go, your resume. I'm surprised you don't have more restaurant experience, what with your aunt running The Diner and all."

"Aunt Myrtle is a believer in making your own way, and I agree. I fill in when she's really busy and did some summer work there during high school, otherwise I make my own way."

"That's impressive and all, but most of your other work is odd jobs in things like construction and some office work." She appeared to be avoiding his gaze as she flipped the page with only a cursory glance at him. "There's little food service experience here."

"I've spent the past few years doing night school to get a degree in business management, which is why I've worked odd jobs. They've kept my schedule flexible enough to go to school and still live on my own. As for food service, I grew up with my aunt and grammy teaching me everything they know in the kitchen. I've even got Grammy's old candy recipes in my arsenal."

For that she put down the resume and met his gaze. An eager grin teased at the corner of her lips and left him distracted for the moment. "Not Grammy Mitchell's prize winning top-secret marshmallow recipes?"

"The one and only." Tag finally relaxed now that he had her full attention. When he leaned back in his seat he offered her a nod. "She left them to me, after she taught me how to make them when I was younger."

"What about Myrtle? Surely she can't be happy to have you using your grandmother's top-secret recipes with the competition."

"I checked with her before I even made up my resume. She says those recipes wouldn't ever make it at The Diner. Only the cakes and pies would mean much to her clientele. Also, they were left to me, and I get to do what I want with them."

"Using bribery to get the job, then?"

"Not bribery. I want to earn the job on my own merits. You were just pointing out my lack of food service experience. I was counter-arguing."

She rewarded him with a large smile and a deep pink flush to her cheeks. "Fair enough. Your letters of reference are hard to ignore, as is your business degree. Still, learning to make candy at your grandma's knee is one thing. Working in a place like this is another."

"I agree. I still say you should give me a shot. I've got plenty of drive and I've loved the concept of this place since I first heard you were putting it together. I know I can handle the business side, and I'm sure I'd be equally capable on the food service side if you gave me a chance."

"I appreciate the argument, and I already had a proposal for you." She leaned her forearms on the desk and clasped her hands together. "A three week trial period."

"Three weeks?" He frowned and shook his head. "That's not much time."

"I don't have much time. Valentine's is coming up and I need to come up with a specialty treat, and make sure I'm well rested. I'm afraid I don't have much time for a settling in period for an assistant manager."

"Three weeks would put me at the first week of February, a two full weeks before Valentine's Day." He leaned forward to meet her straight on. "So give me two months."

"Three weeks at fifteen an hour. One week training on our menu, equipment, and games. Two weeks to see if you and I can work together without killing each other. If we make it through three weeks you can have your two months and a raise."

He couldn't help the grin that formed. "Sounds like a challenge."

"It will be. I'm very particular about my restaurant and I don't like the idea of leaving it in the hands of someone that won't be as particular about it as I am."

"I'll treat it like the most important place on earth." He held out his hand. "I accept your proposal. Three weeks. You won't regret it."

Her small hand folded into his with a warm, soft strength. "I certainly hope I won't. When can you start?"

"This afternoon. Dress code?"

"Casual, but you're working around hot oil so pants are smart. I have men's aprons and hats, so you don't have to wear yellow polka dots."

"I appreciate that." He laughed, keenly aware their hands were still clasped even though their handshake was long over. "I'll be here at one, then? After the lunch hour's over."

"Perfect. I'll have your paperwork ready to fill out and we'll start your training. Welcome to The Midway, Owen."

Owen. No one called him Owen anymore, but he liked the way it sounded when she said it. He liked the way her mouth moved when she said it, too. *Shit, shut up.* He smiled and gave her hand another firm shake, unwilling to release his hold on it yet. "Glad to be here, Miss O'Keefe."

"Oh, please. It's Michaela or Mikey. We're going to be working close together, so Miss O'Keefe is going to get old really fast."

"All right, Michaela it is." He really couldn't stand to call her Mikey, and he wouldn't. "I'll see you in a few hours."

"See you then." Her hand slipped from his and she returned to the files on her desk.

He couldn't see any further reason to stay, so he left the office, wishing he'd had an excuse to stay longer. Then again, he'd be back in a few hours and start working side by side with her for several weeks.

Those daydreams and stray thoughts about her lips, her eyes, her everything would have to stop. If he didn't do well at the job he had a feeling she'd be done with him, period. He didn't get the impression that she trusted much of anyone; it was something he'd have to earn.

He was ready to earn every inch of it, and then maybe he could let those thoughts in again.

All he needed was patience.

Chapter Two

Michaela set her glass of wine on the nightstand and climbed into bed. The sleep medicine her doctor had prescribed was probably a wiser choice over the wine, but after her afternoon working with Owen, she needed the wine more than sleep.

Just as she'd suspected, she'd found him thoroughly distracting, which was the absolute last thing she needed when it came to work. Distraction wouldn't get her business well cared for and maintained in a way that she'd feel safe leaving it in someone else's care.

Still, he'd proven to be a very quick learner. By dinner shift he'd been running the grill and making all of their sandwiches with a flair she almost envied. Apparently his 'occasional' stint at Myrtle's place had given him some good grill experience, so she knew she could trust him behind the line once he knew the menu.

Line work and the sweets side of the business were different, though. Even with his experience with his grandmother, she wondered if he'd be able to handle candy making at the pace she liked. As it stood, she only had two employees able to handle her pace of candy making, and one of them was herself. She could only hope Owen would be up to par.

After that came the business end of it, which made her far more nervous than recipes and candy making. No one touched her finances, not after the mess Gary had made of her life. Having an assistant manager meant she'd have to trust them with the business's money. Settling drawers and the cash-intake, running to the bank, filling out the paperwork, all of it meant he'd both see and have his hand in the financial half of the business.

Right at that moment her phone began to play "Since You've Been Gone" by Kelly Clarkson.

"Speak of the devil," she said, muttering to herself.

She picked up her phone and glared at Gary's name. Rather than answer, she hit the mute button and tossed the phone onto the bed next to her. After long sip of wine, she sank further into the bed to let her thoughts turn back to Owen.

Unfortunately, her phone wasn't done with her and rang again. This time it wasn't Gary's ring tone so she answered without looking at the caller id. "Hello."

"Hey baby, what are you still doing up?" Gary annoyed her with a simple hello, let alone that flower response. Why couldn't he just leave her alone? "You were always an early bird, not a night owl."

No, she went to bed early in the last few years of their marriage to avoid him. She'd already lost him to his many vices, if she'd ever had him at all. She just hadn't figure out how to get out quite yet. "Leave me alone, Gary. I don't want to see you or talk to you. Ever."

"Aw, come on, babe. Ain't you cooled off, yet?"

"Cooled off? From what? Your cheating, your drug abuse, your stealing and deceptions? Which part, exactly, did you expect me to *cool off* from? Because I can promise you I will never cool off from any of it. And stop calling me babe, I hate that."

"Ba-Mikey. I'm a changed man. Give me a shot."

Michaela snorted. "I wouldn't believe that if you showed up with a real halo and angel wings. You're a lying, cheating bastard. My life is better without you in it and I don't ever want to see you again."

"You got someone else, don't you? Who is it, Mikey?"

"You're a fine one to talk."

"Grace wasn't anything to me." His voice warmed into a familiar cajoling tone. The same tone he'd used so many times to get her to forgive him. "That was over years ago."

"Of course it was. You moved on to Sandy, Becky, and Colleen. The day you left was the first day I breathed in a very long time. Just leave me alone. It's not going to happen."

"Sure it is. You're still talking to me now."

She hit the disconnect button and wrinkled her nose at the phone. Once upon a time she'd tried changing her number every time he managed to call her, but she went through too many phone numbers and he always found it again, courtesy of his mother or old friends. A phone number was hard to keep private in a small town like Lake Point.

The phone rang again and she answered. "Leave me the hell alone."

"Sorry," said her friend Eve. "I guess I caught you at a bad time."

"Eve. I'm sorry. Gary was just harassing me via phone. I thought you were him again. Sorry, really, really sorry." Michaela rubbed her forehead with her fingers. "Wish he'd just have stayed gone. I'm too stressed right now to deal with his crap."

"Just try to ignore him. He'll go away again. He always does. If his mother wouldn't keep giving him money he'd never come back."

"Try telling her that." Michaela gulped down the rest of her full glass of wine. "Anyway, let's change the subject before I need to get more wine. My plans for relaxation are pretty much shot anyway."

"I just wanted to see how the first day with Tag went, you lucky dog. Side by side with Tag, must have been lovely."

"It was distracting, not lovely."

"We are in a mood." Eve chuckled. "So you still like him?"

"No, I lust after him. Hard to like a child I hardly know."

"He's no child."

"Don't remind me." Michaela pinched the bridge of her nose. "He's actually a lot more capable than I expected. Jake wasn't lying when he called him a jack of many trades. But that's all, Eve. He's an employee, one that's much younger and I know little about. Besides, I hardly have time to like any man."

"I know. I was hoping having Tag around would give you time to do that. When are we going to go out for a girls night again?"

"Owen's on a trial basis right now. Even if he works out, I won't have time until after Valentine's Day. I've got too much work to do before the Sweethearts On The Square party." Michaela pursed her lips. She still had to come up with a new creation for the theme, and she'd had no luck yet.

"He'll work out. The boy's good. He's going to knock your socks clean off. Maybe the rest of your clothes too."

Michaela laughed until she snorted. She clapped her hand over her nose and tried to settle down. "You're terrible."

"I know, but a girl's gotta dream, you know. Without my imagination and my box of toys I'd have very little in the way of a sex life."

"You'd have a sex life if you tried to shake that ass in your bosses direction."

"This isn't about me and Jake. We already know that's never going to happen." Eve's sharp tone immediately changed. There a pause and then a deep breath from the other end of the line. "Sorry. I didn't mean to snap."

"We have such man troubles," Michaela bemoaned. "I have none, and you can't tell yours how you feel."

"We really need a girls night."

"And a lot more toys."

"And lots and lots of wine."

"Speaking of which, I'm off to get more." Michaela grabbed her glass and rose. "Thanks for cheering me up. I needed it."

"I've never had better timing. Glad I could help."

"You stopping by for lunch tomorrow?"

"I shouldn't. My ass would hate me." Eve sighed. "But I'm craving a tenderloin."

"I'll have one ready, and your ass is fine. Every time we go out guys are checking it out. I wish I had it instead of this bony butt."

"You can have some. I'm a little over-full."

Michaela laughed. "Good night, Eve."

"Nighters."

* * * *

"Michaela?" A warm hand grasped her shoulder and shook gently.

Michaela jolted awake, meeting Owen's concerned face, and blurted, "I'm up, I'm up." She immediately started to straighten the papers on her desk, as if it would cover the fact she was just dreaming about the young man who'd shook her awake. Naughty dreams the likes she'd never had before. Despite her joking with Eve to save face, Michaela considered herself a total prude, but her latest dreams proved that theory wrong.

Dreams of Owen bending her over this very desk and taking her rough, hard, and oh so dirty lingered in her mind and the trickle of sweat that slipped down her nape. She normally wouldn't dare face him while the dreams were still at the forefront, but his chuckle drew her gaze anyway.

He covered his mouth with a hand while leaning against the file cabinets lining the wall.

"I'm awake," she defended before he could even speak. "It was just a cat nap."

"Of course you are." His snort burst from behind his hand and he let out a good loud bark of a laugh. "You have a really cute snore."

"I wasn't—I…" Unfortunately, his laughter was contagious and she found herself joining him before she could form a good argument. She rubbed her face with both hands and groaned. "I'm sorry. I never do that, especially when we're open. I've slept on the couch a couple of times when I had to work late, but to snooze during business hours?"

"You're exhausted. You've got to stop killing yourself." He turned the chair next to her around and straddled it. When he leaned his forearms on the back, she was inevitably drawn to his glorious biceps.

Man, she was so screwed. She gave her head a quick shake to clear it. "It's my business, Owen. I will never stop killing myself for it."

"You need rest, or you'll be no good to the business." He smiled, and set his hand on her wrist she had placed on her desk. "Why don't you go home and take a nap? I'm here now, I'll keep an eye on things and you can be back well before closing. Maybe tonight you'll actually let me help settle the numbers."

Based on all the skill he'd shown in everything she'd thrown at him, she had no doubt he was capable of handling closing the registers and setting the deposit, but the thought still sent a knot of tension right to her stomach. She wrinkled her nose and forced a smile. "Maybe."

"I can't earn your trust if you don't let me try."

"It's not about that."

"Yes, it is. You don't trust easily. If you did you'd have team leads that could close the drawers at night." His grasp loosened on her wrist, and he sighed. "They don't have to even handle anything other than dropping their money into the safe like they would any other cash drop. We, or you, could handle the deposit yourself then the next day."

"Then I wouldn't need you." Even though the thought

of anyone handling the cash turned her stomach, she had to try and cover it with something, even teasing him.

"Yes, you would. I'm irreplaceable."

She grinned and relaxed at his return tease. "I'm not so sure."

"I think you are, you're just afraid to admit it, among other things."

"Is that so?" As much as she wanted to curb the rising blush, she couldn't take her eyes from his. "Anyway, about me leaving, I really shouldn't."

"I think the place will be all right for a couple of hours. You live two blocks away."

"So what were you up to this morning? You're filthy." She'd returned her gaze to his arms; that's how she'd noticed the dark smudges near his elbow and wrist. "Grease?"

"Oil. I thought I got it all." He lifted his arm, his forehead puckering into an adorable hint of a frown. "Damn, don't worry. I'll get good and cleaned up before I touch food. Maybe I should have you check me thoroughly."

A task she sure wouldn't mind for a minute. She managed a laugh to cover the choking lump in her throat and heat the idea sent right to her core. "Cute. Real cute. What were you doing, grease monkey?"

"I was at Cal's working on my Nova."

This time she did choke on her own laughter, and she blinked a few times. "I'm sorry, did you say a Nova? As in a No-Go?"

Owen stopped examining his arms and his gaze snapped to meet hers. "What did you say?"

"A No-Go…are you really working on one?"

"Uh, yeah. I mean, um…"

Michaela couldn't recall a time he'd been at a loss for words, and she liked the change even if it lasted for a second. "What year?"

"A 76 SS. Why?"

Warmth filled her heart and for the first time in a long time, embarrassment was banished to the edge of her mind. "I just can't believe it."

"What?"

"You have to swear not to tell anyone. It'll just perpetuate my nickname worse than it already is."

"Okay." He might have been thoroughly confused, but at least he'd managed a smile when she'd suggested keeping it a secret.

"Good." She rose and closed the office door most of the way before heading to the small file cabinet behind her desk. After unlocking it, she opened it and dug through her too-big purse for her wallet. "Okay, this isn't the best picture. I have several much better ones at home."

Owen rose and turned his chair around to edge closer. Once they were shoulder to shoulder, she showed him the picture. He gasped and snatched the picture from her fingers. "Holy crap."

"That's my dad and me, and my baby. I call her Betty."

"I have never seen her, where do you hide her?" He ran his index finger along the lines of the black Nova in the picture.

"New York winters are assholes to cars, especially beauties like Betty." She leaned in close. "I used to take her out in the summers, but when things with Gary got bad, I didn't want to risk her getting caught in the crossfire."

"Tell me you didn't sell it."

"Technically, I did—but I sold her to Dad. With he and Mom down in Virginia, it wasn't part of the crap-fest of my divorce and she's being well cared for."

"You've been divorced five years. Why not get her back?"

"First couple of years, I didn't care about anything, then this place happened and all my focus has been here." She sighed and took the picture back. "I guess that's part of why I wanted to get an assistant manager. Maybe then I'd have time to get her back."

"Who restored her for you? Looks like an amazing job."

"No one. Dad and I did it all ourselves. From frame to chrome."

"Are you serious?"

"Yup. Dad had some rules about driving and getting a license. I had to be able to change my own oil and tires, I had to know how the engine worked, and I had to learn on a stick before I went to an automatic." She shrugged and offered a smile. With a bit of regret, she slipped the picture back into its place in her wallet. "Turned out, I loved it, but I didn't like to tell anyone. They already called me Mikey. I didn't need to add fuel to the tomboy fire."

"Damn. You just got so much cooler."

"Cooler?" She giggled and nudged his shoulder with her own. When she turned to say something, she realized just how close he was. Embarrassment started to flutter and flap again, rising from the place she'd tried to bury it. She could kiss him now, he was so close, but she couldn't dare for so many reasons. "I'm glad you think so."

"I think more than that." His trademark grin returned and he edged closer. "Like you should get yourself to bed."

With you? Please say with you. She'd officially lost her mind. Owen was her employee and so young, both huge red flags against starting something.

"So are you going?"

"I can't."

"You have to start trusting someone sometime. Trust me for two hours. I swear I'll call you in two hours, but you have to sleep."

The last thing on her mind at that moment was sleep, but it would have to do for now. She finally nodded, "I'll try. I don't do naps well."

"You just had one on your desk. I'm sure you'll do fine."

"Can't I just sleep here on the couch?"

"Let go, Michaela. Trust me."

"Easier said than done."

* * * *

Tag's arms strained with effort as he pulled the wrench to loosen the rusted bolt. He grunted and sagged back onto the concrete. "Still no good, Clay. Sure I shouldn't use the liquid wrench?"

"Won't help your case none." Clay's southern drawl preceded the appearance of him and his ten-gallon hat above the engine Tag struggled with. "Rest your arms and give it another go, or I'll go get the torch."

"Don't put a torch to my girl," Tag protested and shook out his arms. Last thing he wanted was to take a torch to any part of the car, even a rusted bolt. The mere thought renewed his energy and determination. He set the wrench back in place and began to work on his leverage point again. "I'll get it if it kills me."

Clay chuckled. "Thought that might help. Now that I got you pinned down working on Lucy here, you going to give me details on the boss lady?"

The simple mention of Michaela sent a jolt of surprise through him. Tag's fingers slipped off the wrench and it dropped right toward his face. His attempt to bolt out of the way didn't make it and a sharp pain pierced his eyebrow. "Ah, shit."

"You do know you're supposed to hold onto those tools, right?"

"Shut up." Tag kept his eyes screwed shut, rubbing his eyebrow. Without a doubt there'd be a good knot there soon.

"Dang. Knew you liked her, but if just talking about her makes you forget how to handle a tool, you're farther gone than I thought." Clay's footsteps circled the car and came to a stop near Tag's legs. "She's a beauty, but more my age than yours."

"You're only four years older than me."

"She's ten years older than you." Laughter cut through the whir of wheels against concrete. By the time the pain subsided enough for Tag to open his eyes, Clay was next to him on another backboard under the engine. "Still, can't say as I blame you."

"I had a huge crush on her when I was a teen," Tag admitted. While he fished for the wrench, he avoided Clay. He needn't have worried since Clay was fiddling with another bolt. "And she's my boss."

"And you still got the hots for her."

Tag couldn't deny it if he'd tried. The simple crush had

been getting worse since he'd learned about her car. The cool detachment she'd shown him since hiring him had faded into warmth and a growing friendship, which made him like her even more. "I wouldn't say it like that."

"So what, then?"

"She's not what I expected." After years of crushing on her from a distance, the truth proved better than liking the red head with shocking blue eyes. Now he knew about her quiet sense of humor, and her love of cars. "Man, I knew her as my babysitter's friend. She was hot and way older. Now, she's not just some long-distance crush."

Clay didn't respond at first, and when Tag looked over, the man's features were scrunched up and red from effort.

Tag burst out laughing, "Just a bit of elbow grease, huh?"

"Smart…" Clay grunted and released his grip long enough to readjust. "Aleck."

"Hey, you're the one teasing me about taking a torch to my baby." Tag set his own wrench and resumed work on the bolt he'd been working on.

"We'll get it." The cowboy hat toppled to the ground and Clay pushed it away before he wiped his forehead. "May take a week for each bolt, but you don't have a timetable or nothing."

"I'd rather it be done this century." Tag gave another shove on the wrench.

"You'll never manage it that way." Michaela's voice shocked both men into jumping.

Tools clanged against cement, and Tag jumped so high, he hit his forehead on the bolt, in the exact spot the wrench had clocked him minutes ago. "Ow, damn it. Son of a—"

Michaela giggled, a foreign sound to Tag's ears, but so welcome it almost overrode his pain. Almost. "Didn't mean to scare you guys, I thought you heard me walking in."

"Not even a little bit." Tag pressed the heel of his hand against his eyebrow. "I think I'm going to have to call in. I might have a concussion after that."

"You're wearing protective goggles, and you still managed to get hurt?" A foot nudged his leg, and Michaela granted him the pleasure of another laugh. "That takes skill."

"It hit right above the goggles, the second time today." Tag pushed against the floor to roll out from under the car. "I think it's time to give her what she wants. Clearly, she doesn't want me pestering her today."

Michaela hissed and knelt in front of him. She touched his forehead and swept some hair aside. "That does look painful. Have any ice packs in your first aid kit, Clay?"

"Think so. If not, I got ice upstairs in the apartment. Let me look." Clay rolled out from under the car and got to his feet.

As Clay hopped up the steps toward his office, Michaela turned back to Tag. Her brows puckered as she lifted the goggles from his face. "You're going to have one hell of a goose egg."

"If the headache is any indication, I don't doubt it." Tag scrunched his nose and raised his finger to touch his eyebrow. All of his efforts to not flinch were wasted when a sharp stab of pain radiated under his probing fingers. "I'm not usually such a klutz."

"Of course not." Her lips twitched as she sat down on the floor next to him. She wiped her hands on her jeans before she dug through her huge purse. "I always carry aspirin in here. I think I have some water, too."

"Here you go." Clay approached with the first aid kit. "Got just about anything you might need in here. Ice packs, alcohol swabs, band-aids. Momma always said there was nothing that worked more than kissing it to make it better, though. 'Scuse me now, Mrs. Neeley just came in for an oil change."

Michaela might have ducked her head in an attempt to cover any blush, but Tag saw it anyway. She shook her head and set the kit on the floor between their legs. "We'll get you cleaned up after you've had some aspirin."

Tag held out his hand obediently when she shook the bottle at him. If nothing else, the recent weeks had taught him not to push his luck when she was overtly embarrassed. Those were the times when her fiery red-headed temper showed the most. Well, then and when someone even hinted at breaching even a minor trust. "Yes, ma'am."

"Ugh. Owen, really."

He offered a grin that had always won him points when he was in trouble with a woman. With one corner of his mouth quirked up he intentionally closed his fingers over hers on the water bottle. "You give me orders, I call you ma'am."

"I am your boss."

"I'm off the clock."

"So am I."

"You can still boss me around." The words came out before he could stop them, and she ducked her head again. He tossed back the aspirin and chugged the water. His head rang in reaction to how quick he'd thrown his head back, but he forced his way through it. "So what are you doing here anyway?"

"I wanted to see the car."

"But—I mean, what are you doing away from the shop?"

She lifted her head, the hints of embarrassment faded into delicate rosy cheeks. One eyebrow lifted and she smirked. "I do leave from time to time."

"Do not."

"It's only nine in the morning. I'm not open and no one comes in until ten-thirty."

"And that's when you do paperwork." He chuckled, even though it made his head swim. "You really wanted to see this beast?"

"She's pretty rough, but yes I did." She scooted closer and ripped open an alcohol swab. "I know Clay has connections, but I can give you the name of the best paint guy I know."

Tag jumped again when she made contact with the impact point and the cold sting of antiseptic buzzed through his sore head. Air hissed through his clenched teeth, and he took a few deep steadying breaths to relax his jaw. "How bad is it cut?"

"Not too bad, but that bolt was pretty rusty I'm guessing, if the struggle you two were having was any indication. Even if you cleaned them first, you didn't get it all. You'll have to keep an eye on it, and maybe go see Doc anyway." She was close enough to distract him from the pain now.

His fingers twitched with the urge to touch her, but he held still and let her clean his wound. For his part, he stared at her neck, because he figured it was safer than staring at her lips, or her perky tits that hovered at the edge of his vision. "Shit," he muttered.

"Almost done." Her misinterpretation probably saved his neck in this case. "If you do need tonight off, it's okay. It is my fault, after all."

"You're not getting out of giving me vault control tonight that easy."

She pursed her lips and returned her attention to the first aid kit. "You're not funny."

"I'm a little funny."

"Not really."

"You have to say I am. I'm injured, see?" He pointed to his forehead and pushed his lip out in a pout. "Owie."

Even with the amount of self-control he knew she had, she snorted. "You poor baby."

"I really am. The car hurt me. It was horrible."

"With this behavior maybe you don't deserve the night off."

"Probably not, but you do."

"Stop that." She lifted the bandage toward him. When he grasped her wrists to stop her, she blanched. "Owen?"

"You do. And after this, so do I. What do you say next week, once we get Barbara set up to lead the closing shift, we go have some fun?"

"F—fun?"

"A hockey game. I can get us good seats and you can remember what it means to relax and have a good time." He smiled and sat up closer. "Come on. It'll give you a chance to see that the place won't burn down without us, and what's more fun than a hockey game with a good friend?"

"I haven't been to a hockey game in years." She

worried her lip between her teeth. "But I just got you trained, and the deal wasn't that we'd leave the place without at least one of us there."

The headache didn't make him dizzy enough to lose his good sense, or else he might have plucked her lip right out from between her teeth. Instead, he grabbed an ice compress to keep his hands busy. Once he popped the inner bubble and got the compress started, he placed it to his forehead. "And what did I tell you about trusting people?"

"I'm not good at that."

"I noticed." He nudged her hip with his knee. "We'll do a game in the middle of the week, so the place will be slow. Brenda can just drop the cash in the vault and we can go to the store after the game to check and make sure it all balances."

She frowned and her brows twitched toward another pucker. "You're not letting me argue."

"Because I don't plan on letting you say no. When's the last time you went out and just had fun?"

"High school."

"That's it, we're going. Wednesday."

"Wednesday?" She started to replace the unused items in the first aid kit, setting aside the gauze. "I don't know. Is there even a game?"

"I'm sorry, do you live here? Do you have to ask?" Tag poked her thigh and snorted. The flash of pain from his sharp snort made him wince. "Ow. Anyway, you know there's a game Wednesday, I know you do. You have the team's schedule posted next to the staff's schedules. I've heard you talk hockey with Cash Stawski."

"That's because Cash plays hockey, he's trying out for

the team." She scooted closer with the gauze and antibiotic ointment. "And you're right. I know there's a game, just like everyone in town knows Buffalo's, Rochester's, and the pee-wee league game schedules. I'm trying to back out gracefully."

He pointed to what he assumed was a growing lump on his forehead. "I'll play the guilt card if I have to."

A smile started to light her features and she touched the ice pack he still held there. It was a simple gesture that made him wish she was touching him instead. "Fine. I hope I don't regret this."

"Trust me, you won't."

"You keep asking me to trust you."

"I keep hoping you'll learn to."

Chapter Three

There was just over two weeks until the Sweetheart's On The Square Party, and Michaela still had nothing to bring to it. Or rather, she had a few of the recipes Owen had added to the mix especially for the holiday that were already selling like hot cakes, but none of them were what she needed.

"Any luck?" Deanna Parker, the assistant town manager, and an old friend of Michaela's, sat down with her coffee. The shop was blissfully quiet at the moment, letting them have their meeting outside of the chaos in Michaela's office.

"No. Nothing is quite right." Michaela rubbed her forehead with her fingers. "The recipes from Grammy Montague are a great boost, but I have yet to figure out something just perfect for the holiday that hasn't already been done. I mean, the recipes are good, but they're nothing new."

"You do know you're making a bigger deal of this than it needs to be." Deanna sipped her coffee. "So long as you're bringing some of your famous treats, and some of Grammy's, the party-goers are going to be in heaven."

"Maybe so, but I really wanted something new." Michaela shook her head and closed the recipe book. "Let's talk about the party itself. I still don't know why I signed up to help with all of this. I must have been insane."

"Because long as I've known you, you've taken on more than you can chew. You did take on Gary, after all. This party is no exception"

"Don't remind me. It's bad enough he's in town."

Deanna set her hand on Michaela's. "Just so long as you aren't thinking about going back to him, it doesn't matter. I'd hate to lose you as a friend again."

Like most of her friends, Deanna had been erased from her life after she'd married Gary. They all tried for a while, but Michaela now admitted she'd been embarrassed after the pregnancy had turned out to be a false positive, and when the painful reason behind the false positive had been revealed, Michaela had all but retreated from life. In some ways she supposed that made it even easier for Gary to be the slime he was. He certainly hadn't wanted Michaela standing up for herself. She sighed. "Trust me, the last thing I want is to get back with Gary."

"Good." Deanna patted her hand, oblivious to the turmoil she'd caused in Michaela's head and heart. "Then again, I don't blame you with eye candy around. Eve says she thinks it's going well. Is she right?"

"He's much more capable than I expected. I had no idea he had a degree in business management, but he's proved it in spades." Even though it almost physically hurt to leave the building and let him handle closing the vault, Michaela had done it the night before. When she'd arrived this morning, everything was in its place and all evidence of the paperwork was in place.

"I don't know how you do it. I'd be far too distracted to work alongside him."

"He's an employee. A friend, and an employee. I am an adult and I can keep my hormones in check, thank you." Michaela didn't dare admit how difficult it really was, especially with the looming hockey game in a couple of days. There was also the pesky, nagging feeling that Owen was flirting with her. She kept trying to convince herself it was her imagination, that she'd been the only one affected when she'd helped him with his hurt forehead.

"I know, but still." Deanna sighed and shook her head. "Anyway. We were talking about Sweethearts On The Square."

"We were supposed to be, yes." Michaela shoved off the melancholy and emotional confusion as best she could and forced a laugh. "So let's do that and stop picking on me for hiring a capable assistant manager."

"With an ass that won't quit."

"Dee-dee."

"Sorry." Deanna winked and turned back to the folder she'd set on the table. "Hey, he's more than enough to make me want to swing both ways, and I don't say that about any man."

"Terrible." Michaela leaned forward and steered the direction back to the party instead of Owen's considerable assets. It worked until Owen himself showed up an hour later. After that, she was able to blame Deanna's distraction, even though it was her own that did the whole planning session in. She rose and gathered her papers. "So the next group meeting is at eight Wednesday morning, right?"

"Right. You'll make it this time, won't you?" Deanna quirked a brow. "I don't mind meeting with you and catching you up and getting your ideas this way, but the rest of the committee would really like to know you are actually participating."

"I promise I'll be there. Owen will open on Wednesday in case it runs over." Michaela hoped she hadn't physically flinched at the nervous jolt in her stomach over the idea. "After all, that's what I hired him for."

"I would have hired him for his ass alone." Deanne winked again before slipping away and outside.

Michaela sighed and rubbed her temples. Every single one of her friends reveled in teasing her about Owen being so close all the time. It certainly didn't help her own state of distraction, and the sudden jump in hormones she'd been certain were long dead after Gary.

Of course, she could only imagine the whispers that would erupt if her impossible imaginings came true. He was ten years her junior, after all. "Here's to you, Mrs. Robinson," she muttered under her breath.

"What was that?" Owen spun the chair across from her around and straddled it. He leaned his forearms on the back of the chair. Every simple, innocent move me made nearly drove her to distraction. Damn him. "You okay? Or did I mess up last night?"

"What?" She blinked a few times and shook her head. "Oh, no. I'm sorry. The Valentine's preparations are just wiping me out. I might have been home last night, but it wasn't a very restful night. You did fine, Owen. Actually, I was impressed with the state of this place when I came in. So, thank you."

With every word he'd brightened more, until a beaming smile warmed over half the doubts right out of her cold heart. "So do I get a passing grade?"

She chuckled and shook her head. "This isn't school."

"Too bad."

"What? Why?"

"Because then I could start singing 'Hot for Teacher'."

"Oh my God." She buried her face in her hands, the tingling burn of a blush creeping up from head to toe. "Owen!"

He laughed and scooted his chair close enough to nudge her. "You're supposed to laugh. Although, I enjoy the blushing more, I think."

"You're terrible. Trying to make me blush is just mean." Even worse that his only goal was to get a rise out of her. She'd been right, she was imagining the flirting. Being more embarrassed at this point would never be possible.

"The blushing is just a bonus." He winked and leaned closer. "Promise."

Dear Heavens he was going to kill her with this teasing. She cleared her throat and gathered her papers, trying to pull her gaze from his face. "Why don't we go into the office and discuss ending your probationary status, and making your assistant manager status permanent."

"Happy to, boss." He rose and took the extra step of holding her chair as she got up with an armload of papers. "Can I help?"

"I got them, thanks." She tried to smile, but figured it was best to avoid eye contact until the last of her embarrassment waned. If it ever did.

* * * *

Tag mentally kicked himself all the way back to Michaela's office. While he'd tried to laugh it off, he knew he'd crossed the line with the 'Hot for Teacher' comment. What had he been thinking?

Absolutely nothing.

Or rather, nothing at all appropriate for a work situation, or his boss, or right in front of the staff, even if they couldn't hear him just then. She'd just been casting him looks during her meeting with Deanna, and then her compliment had boosted his spirits and loosened his tongue.

He knew her ex was a piece of work and if half the rumors were true, she had plenty of reason to not trust much of anyone. Still, he'd thought he was making progress and prayed he hadn't messed it up with his misstep—whether he'd meant it or not.

"I'm really sorry about that comment," he started as soon as they stepped in the office. "That was inappropriate, no matter my intention."

"Oh." The pink hue hadn't quite left her cheeks and now she managed to meet his gaze with her bright blue eyes. "Oh, it's fine."

"No, it's not. I like you." The blush deepened, and he couldn't stop his grin and inner hope she liked him back. "I have to confess so you maybe can forgive me."

"There's nothing to forgive, Owen. You were teasing me. Unfortunately, I'm very bad at taking a joke." She dropped into her chair and bent over to unlock her personnel drawer. If it wasn't a dismissal, he didn't know what was.

"I'm still sorry. I shouldn't have—"

"It's fine." She snapped and slammed the drawer shut, slapping the file she'd removed onto the desk. "Don't beat a dead horse. Now sit, please. We came in here to discuss your probationary period, and what I think."

Damn, he had messed up. Somehow he had to fix it, preferably before the hockey game on Wednesday. He sat as directed and nodded slowly. "All right."

"Despite my initial concerns, I have to admit that you've done better than I'd hoped." She flipped open the folder and then leaned her forearms on the desk. "So I'm lifting your probation, effective immediately. I'll make sure your promised raise also takes effect starting with today's wages."

He grinned, regretting it when her gaze immediately dropped to the folder. "That's great. I'm glad I was able to prove my capabilities to you with your tough expectations."

"If they weren't tough, I wouldn't be able to trust you to run the shop in my absence. As it stands, you'll be opening alone on Wednesday. I have a meeting."

"For the Sweethearts On The Square. Right. Is there anything special you need done?"

"I was hoping to get the ring toss game changed out that day. If you have time, I'd like to have it switched into the rubber duck river. The kids swarm to that one, and we haven't had a kid friendly game since Thanksgiving." She closed her folder and sighed. "That'll free me up to work on the Sweethearts party and all of the headaches that entails."

"I've put a fresh supply of ibuprofen in the first aid kit."

Even though she still wouldn't look at him, she finally cracked a smile. "I guess you think of everything. Thanks."

"Not everything, but I try." He sat forward. "Is there anything I can do to help with any of it? I've got Carrie and Madeline working exclusively on making and wrapping the sweets for the booth today and tomorrow. I figured the sooner they were done, the better. It'll be one last thing to worry about in the rush to get to the finish line."

Her shoulders dropped and she shook her head. "You need to stop. I don't know what to do without something to worry about."

"I think they call it relaxing."

There it was again, a hint of a smile she tried to wipe away. "Owen."

"Part of my job is to be here to make your life easier. Remember, you haven't had a day off in a long time. That's the goal."

"Not sure it will ever happen."

He wanted nothing more than to go to her side and comfort her, but he'd already crossed too many lines today. "I think you're just used to the stress. And the lack of a life. And being able to have the shop as your armor against any battle—it is the perfect excuse for anything."

"I made this place. It is all I have, and I'm going to make sure it succeeds." Pain lanced her words, and not for the first time, when she called the shop all she had.

He frowned and shook his head. "It isn't all you have. You've got friends. Family. A sweet car that you need to get back up here so I can see it."

Mentioning Betty had the effect he'd hoped for, and the bright smile returned to her features. "No fair playing the Nova card."

"It got you to smile. That's all that matters." And it was.

* * * *

Michaela gripped the phone buried in her coat pocket. She had no idea why she'd agreed to this. Her nose was cold, her toes were frozen, and she was nervous and fidgety and really, desperately wanted to check in on the shop again. Even though the game hadn't started yet, the crowd in the arena performed the wave all the way around. She couldn't bring herself to take part, though; her mind was back on The Midway.

"Here you go. One light beer." Tag handed her a drink. "I got some nachos, a couple of hot dogs, some cotton candy and—"

"My God, Owen. What did you do, buy out the concession stand? I can't even see your face." She set down her beer in the cup holder and rose. From the top of the stack in his arms she grabbed the unsteady hot dogs and nachos off of the huge tub of popcorn.

He grinned and shrugged, nearly knocking over the popcorn and his own beer in the process. "I wanted to make sure we were set for the rest of the game. Now we just have to catch a beer vendor if we want more. I've even got some subs in this box."

When he lifted his hands she could see the box under the popcorn tub. In spite of herself, she laughed. "You're insane, you know that?"

"I do. At least I know you can smile. I haven't seen that in days."

"Valentine's Day is in two weeks and I still haven't come up with a good special candy for the holiday. Speaking of which, I should call."

"No. No shop-talk tonight. You agreed. You can't call, you can't text, you're supposed to be enjoying yourself. I mean, come on. Look at these seats. Jake has the best season tickets, right in the neutral zone." He managed to sit and settled the popcorn on the floor between them. "Now let me see your phone."

"Oh no. You aren't taking my phone." She stuck her hand back in her pocket. "Not a chance. What if something happens?"

"Brenda and I had a long talk this afternoon. She has my number, and she'll be calling me if there's anything wrong."

"No."

"Kayla."

Her protest died on her lips, and her heart skipped a beat of its own accord. "What did you call me?"

"Sorry."

"No. Don't be." The familiar heat of a blush crept up her neck and she lifted her beer as a distraction. At least it was cold, and she could pass off the blush to the temperature. "I just don't know anyone that's ever called me that before. It's always Mikey."

"I never liked that."

"And I never liked Tag." She sighed and leaned back in her seat.

"I promised you a night off, a night to relax. That's what this is supposed to be about. You haven't had a night off in three years. You've barely slept in the past year. Will you please give me your phone?"

"I don't like this." She begrudgingly pulled the phone out of her pocket. "But I do like the thought of relaxing for a change."

"Good." He took the phone and set it in his own pocket.

When he opened his mouth next, the loud blare of the goal horn got the crowd on their feet to welcome the teams onto the ice. He shrugged and leaned in. "It's not my favorite way to relax, but it'll do."

This time the fire of embarrassment climbed up her cheeks. Michaela ducked down in her seat and pulled the collar of her coat up high to cover it as best as she could. Once she realized she was the only person sitting in the general area and Owen had turned a raised eyebrow on her, she leaped to her feet. "Sorry."

He laughed and bumped her hip with his. "No worries. Just have fun." As the announcer welcomed the home team, Owen lifted his fingers to his mouth and blew out a sharp whistle.

Much as she hated to admit it, he was right. Years had passed since the last time she'd relaxed. Certainly since she'd just forgotten about everything else and let go to have real fun. Maybe she could let go for tonight. Maybe.

"I told you." Owen spoke into her ear, so close his warm breath brushed along her ear lobe in a caress that shouldn't have been so exciting. "We'll go to the store after the game. I have my phone. You don't have to worry."

When his hand grasped her elbow, warm and supportive, she turned toward him. While her imaginings of his flirtatious nature were just that, she knew without a doubt now that he was, if nothing else, her friend—and a good assistant manager. She had to start trusting some time.

"We good?" His brows lifted, and his face hovered near hers. The crowd around them disappeared in the warm smile he gave her. "Kayla?"

She let her shoulders drop in attempt to brush aside the

tension before she returned his smile. With a wink she turned back toward the ice and lifted her own fingers to her lips. As her dad had taught her, she fit them in place and blew. Her whistle rivaled those around her and she cheered on the team before leaning toward him again. "We're more than good."

They sat in unison after the starting lineup was announced and the teams began to warm up. Owen lifted the bucket of popcorn off the floor and held it between them. "So are you a fan, or do I have to explain anything?"

"Do you think the girls you date actually need an explanation, or do they just want you close, whispering in their ear?" She leaned her elbow on the armrest and set her chin on her fist. The levels of confusion and denial that crossed his features, followed by the final settling of his lips into a pout shouldn't have made her so pleased, but it did. It was good to give back the teasing he'd been throwing her way for a bit.

"Wait. No, you can't be serious."

"We live just outside of Rochester, across the lake from Canada, and just over an hour from one major league hockey team. Every girl in Lake Point has some knowledge of hockey. Whether their brothers played it, they played it, their fathers played it or watch every single game on satellite TV," she finally admitted.

"I'll be damned."

She grinned. "If it makes you feel better, you can help me along in my understanding through the game. Like what are those circles for on the ice?" With wide eyes, she batted her lashes at him.

"You aren't funny."

"Then why are you smiling?"

"Because…I don't know." There was no way on earth Owen was actually blushing, even if it sure appeared so with the ruddy red filling his cheeks. He turned and drank down half his beer in one gulp. "I didn't think I was that naïve."

"Don't blame yourself. Women play terrible games sometimes thinking it will get them a man. I gave up on games some time ago, but I know many that haven't. I just can't figure out if it gets worse or better once they're married."

His hand settled on hers, and the warmth of his touch radiated right through her glove. "Maturity is hard to come by, I hear. That's what Auntie-M tells me."

"Myrtle is smart."

"She says you have to live through some shit to get there."

"Boy, do you ever." Melancholy swept through her heart like the cold air of the rink seeping into her lungs. Only his hand on hers felt warm, and she grasped onto it.

The blare of the goal horn startled them both out of the moment and their hands separated to clap as they rose to their feet. The game was about to start, and it would be best for her to stay in the game now.

* * * *

The game had done everything Tag hoped it would, and more. Somehow, for one night, Kayla had relaxed, had fun, and even stooped to teasing him on multiple occasions. He couldn't remember a thing about the game; his mind filled with images of her.

The sweet curve of her ass when she'd jumped up to

cheer on a score, or even better, a fight, had left him unable to stand on a few occasions for all the ideas it gave him. The way her smile lit up her whole face warmed his heart. For once he'd seen the way she was before her world changed. Whatever had changed it was more than just Gary.

Although if all the stories he'd heard about Gary were true, he couldn't blame her for being broken. Still, something in those gorgeous blue eyes echoed of a deeper pain. One beyond Gary.

A sharp whistle and the wave of her glove in his face shook him out of his reverie. "Owen, you in there?"

"Yeah, sorry. You were in the bathroom forever."

"I know. It's obscene. I was about to skip out of line and head into the men's room. I forgot that's the one reason I hate going to games. It's worse now that I'm old enough to drink, and just older in general."

"You're not old."

She snorted and zipped her coat, falling into step beside him on the walk back to his truck. "I'm ten years older than you. Trust me, I'm old."

"That's just a number. It doesn't mean anything. I don't know anyone that acts their age. Some behave like they're far younger, some like they're far older. Uncle Peter was fifteen years younger than Auntie-M. He still died when I was only six." He shrugged. "Age doesn't mean anything. It's how we act that does."

"I didn't know you felt so strongly about that." Her voice was barely a whisper. He almost didn't hear it over the cheers and whistles of the fans returning to their cars.

"Well, I do." He glanced at her. "You never let me make my confession."

"Confessions are overrated."

"Too bad. I want you to hear it."

"That's the problem. Confession might be good for your soul, but that doesn't mean it is for mine, or that I want to hear it." Her shoulders hunched until he couldn't see her features past the collar of her coat. "The last confession I heard ended my marriage, and pretty much my life at the time. I don't care for confessions."

"Hey." He caught her by the elbow and stopped her increasing pace. Once she'd finally turned to face him, he smiled. "This is nothing like that."

"Are you sure?"

"Pretty sure."

"If you're telling me you're quitting because I'm such a—"

"What? No." Tag pulled her closer and caught her other elbow so she had to face him. "I am not about to quit on you. I like my job, and I like you. Probably more than I should."

"I…What?" Whether she meant to or not, her hands wrapped around his forearms and held tight like she feared falling over.

"It's terrible. You're my boss. Kayla, I know that. And I had a crush on you for years before you ever hired me. But getting to know you, the real you, when you let me in, changed that. I don't think it's a crush any longer."

"This isn't nice," she whispered. Tears glimmered at the edge of her eyes. When she blinked, several shimmered on her long lashes. "Don't tease me like that."

"I'm not teasing." He released one of her elbows to brush aside a tear with his thumb. "That 'Hot for Teacher' line was crass and stupid. It also wasn't entirely true. Yeah,

I'm hot for teacher, but I'm more impressed with who you are."

"You don't—you can't—I…" She took several deep breaths and her eyes fluttered closed. After a moment she let out a choked laugh. "I can't even form a sentence."

"You just did." The breath he'd been holding released when she laughed in reply. "I'm sorry. Maybe I shouldn't have—"

"Eve and I used to call you jail bait." In a good sign, she still hadn't released her grip on his arm, and she hadn't moved away. "I knew it was dangerous hiring you. I just didn't realize that it was dangerous because of more than your looks. I think you're a good guy. I honestly didn't believe those existed."

"I'm glad you see me that way. Is there a 'but' to that statement?"

"Let me count the ways." She took a deep breath, and started talking fast. "I'm ten years older; I'm seriously messed up; I don't trust anyone, not even my friends. I'm also not very good at relationships. Never was. Just because I was married means nothing. In fact, it might have made me worse. And last, but not least, I am your boss and I can't get sued for sexual harassment. I have no money."

"Breathe, Kayla." He released her other elbow and wrapped his arms fully around her. "First off, I told you age doesn't matter. Second, I know you don't trust easy, and I know you're messed up. Third, no relationship is the same. Lastly, I am not going to sue you. If anything I was harassing you a little bit."

"So you were flirting with me? All this time?"

"You bet your sweet little ass I was."

"This could be a really huge mistake, Owen. I don't know that I can handle any more of those in my life." Her lips drew together in a small 'O' and she blew out a long breath.

"It could be, but how about this? It's not a relationship. We'll just take it a day at a time and see where it goes. If it doesn't work, it doesn't."

"I'm really messed up. So much more than you know. You've got so much ahead of you. You shouldn't be thinking about trying anything with someone so jaded."

"Maybe I like that you're jaded."

Her forehead puckered. "Then you're messed up."

"So we'll be messed up together." He was rewarded with the sweet sound of her laugh. With one finger hooked under her chin, he tilted her head up. "We'll try. All I ask is if you have a problem, tell me—and give me the benefit of the doubt."

"I'll promise to try."

"I'll take it for now." He bent toward her, close enough to hear her sharp intake of breath when he got close to her lips. A smile took over in the instant before he pulled her into a slow, soft kiss.

Her lips were soft and inviting, drawing him after only a moment's hesitation. The sweet taste of cotton candy lingered, and he brushed his tongue across the seam of her lips. Her small gasp granted him the chance he wanted and he swept his tongue through her warm mouth.

The cold chill of the evening was replaced with growing warmth as her arms wrapped around him and she relaxed against his body. Her every response to his kiss was tentative, and he tried to keep himself in check, even as each simple brush of her tongue against his drove him crazy with need.

He retreated slowly from the sweet taste of cotton candy and strawberries that was her kiss and pressed his forehead to hers. "I've wanted to do that for a long time."

"The feeling's mutual."

"What else have you wanted to do?" Once again he was rewarded with the deep hues of a blush. "God, you're gorgeous when you blush."

"No, I'm not."

"Yes, you are. Why do you think I try to make it happen so much?"

She bit her lips and shook her head.

"At least now I know I'm not the only one with fantasies."

Chapter Four

The apartment was oddly silent. Michaela wasn't used to be home before The Midway closed, but she'd given the closing shift to Owen. He'd promised to call when the night was done with an update.

For a few fleeting hours that afternoon she'd worked alongside him, cleaning the office and setting up schedules for the coming month. Every minute had been pure distraction, as her mind kept drifting back to the hockey game the night before.

Her lips still tingled from the soft, sweet kiss. She didn't know how to admit to him that she felt like a total prude, and completely incapable of a physical relationship no matter how much she wanted one. She'd not had sex since—goodness, her first year of marriage.

No, that wasn't entirely true. There were a few occasions where Gary had forced the marriage card and she'd given in. Still, she didn't know the first thing about anything beyond the basics. For her, sex had never been good or exciting, but every time she caught a flirtatious smile from Owen she craved it.

Craved, wanted. She was almost desperate.

"Who are you kidding? You are desperate, you fool." She poured herself another glass of wine and sipped at it. Maybe she should call Eve and admit her failings and lack of experience. Eve wouldn't judge her. Maybe.

She groaned and dropped her forehead to the counter. "I'm such an idiot."

Distraction. That's what she needed, simple distraction. She fumbled along the counter to her remote and hit the power button. The TV flickered to life, only to make her more miserable with the sweet, romantic kiss being shared by the characters on the screen.

She flipped through several channels, but sappy movie after sappy movie appeared. "Valentine's Day—the perfect excuse to air every romantic comedy that ever existed."

The doorbell cut through her musings, and she gladly turned off the TV. She frowned and glanced at the clock. Who would stop by at almost eleven at night?

She slipped off the stool and crept to the door, unease twisted her stomach. After the visits and phone calls the past few weeks, she had a bad feeling it might be Gary. Instead, she found Owen's features in the keyhole. "Owen?"

"Uh, yeah. Hi, Kayla. Can you let me in? It's cold out here."

"Oh. Oh, right." She fumbled with the lock and pulled open the door. A blast of cold air fairly shoved Owen right inside. With a shiver, she shoved the door closed and locked it again. "Brrr. Sorry, I was expecting you to call."

"I know, but I have something for you I think you're going to like."

"What?" When he leaned in and kissed her gently, she flushed. "Was that it?"

"Okay, so I have two things." He chuckled and lifted a basket she recognized from the store. "I have your Valentine's Party treat."

"Are you serious?" She eyed the basket and pointed to the kitchen. "If you're serious, you might have just made my whole weekend."

"I might make it anyway." A seductive husky note added to the flirting, and sent a shiver down her spine. "Now, this treat is mostly my own creation. I do use Grammy's marshmallow recipe for a bit of it, though."

"Marshmallows?" She followed him into the kitchen. When he lifted the basket's lid, she tried to peek in.

"Please tell me you have a fryer here." He pulled three containers and one of their chocolate drizzler's out. Once they were on the counter, he turned and offered that adorable cock-eyed grin. "I couldn't fit a whole fryer in my pants."

She giggled and turned to open a cabinet near the dishwasher. "If you'd tried, you might have been met with unfortunate consequences."

"Ow times infinity," He grunted, and she heard him opening the plastic containers. "I would have said something about this sooner, but it was just an idea. I wanted to test it before I got your hopes up."

With the small fryer in hand, she returned to the counter. Once she'd plugged it in, she scooted around him to inspect his assembly line. Lollipop sticks, heart shaped red marshmallows, egg whites? She raised her eyebrows and moved on, graham cracker crumbs. "Okay. I give up. What on earth are you making?"

"I call them Deep-Fried Sweethearts."

"I like it already. But you're frying marshmallows?"

"Yup." He adjusted the heat on the fryer and rubbed his hands together. "It'll take about fifteen minutes for that to heat up. In the meantime, there's something else I need to do."

Before Michaela could fully process what was happening, he backed her against the opposite counter. He gripped her hips and lifted her like she weighed nothing. The second her butt landed on the counter, he moved between her legs.

"Don't look so surprised." His warm chuckle teased along her neck when he placed a kiss there. A kiss that sent a jolt of excitement right to her core, unlike anything she'd ever experienced. "Do I need to start singing?"

"Oh God, please don't." She laughed, and tried to relax to enjoy the moment. Every inch of her skin tingled in an almost painful mix of pleasure and embarrassment. She took a shaky breath and whispered, "Owen."

"Hm?" Soft kisses danced along her jugular, while his fingers tiptoed along her thighs.

"Wait." With no small amount of regret, she pushed him back a few inches. "This is really…it's embarrassing for me to say. But you should be warned."

"What?" His brow furrowed and he flattened his palms on her thighs. The teasing was immediately replaced with concern. God, he was sweet.

"I—well, I sort of suck in bed."

Jaw slack, he blinked rapidly for several seconds. When he clamped his jaw shut, it was immediately clear he was trying not to laugh.

She tensed and tried to shimmy away. Unfortunately, he held her firm where she was. "I said it was embarrassing, I don't need to be laughed at. Please, let me go."

"No, you don't go anywhere." Even now he couldn't keep the laughter from his voice. "You're totally misunderstanding."

"You're laughing. At me. What's to misunderstand?"

"I'm not laughing at you—okay, maybe a little, but only because I think it's absolutely ridiculous that you'd think you suck in bed." He still refused to let go of her legs. "Kayla, why on earth would you think that?"

"I don't think it, I know it. I'm an A-1 prude. I've only been with a few guys, and it was never good. It has to be me."

"Or—it was them."

"Sure. Whatever you say. But I'm the common denominator, and even talking about this is embarrassing. Please, let me go." Her face was literally on fire, it had to be. She buried her cheeks in her hands and was sure her palms would burn off. "I just don't want you to have expectations."

"Kayla." His voice was soft and one hand lifted from her leg. Moments later she felt a gentle brush along her collar bone. Tingles followed behind, and once again the hint of pleasure made her crave him. "Do you like it when I touch you, or kiss you?"

She groaned and tried to disappear into her own hands. Was it possible to die from complete embarrassment? She sure as hell was going to try.

"I don't ever want you to be embarrassed around me. I'm sorry I laughed, but I have a feeling it's you that has been gypped out of the real fun—not the guys you were with."

A soft sigh slipped out when he began to massage her neck with one hand. "I'm sorry. You must think I'm an idiot. To be embarrassed just to talk about it."

"No. Not an idiot. Just someone who really needs to

know a good time." He gently pried her hands from her face and met her gaze. "I appreciate you telling me the truth. I just hope you'll let me prove you wrong."

"I guess I wouldn't mind trying." Hell, she'd love to try. She just loathed the thought of disappointing him. She set her hands on his chest when he leaned in. "After the Deep-Fried Sweethearts."

"Oh, right. Damn. You got me all hot and bothered, I forgot all about those."

"A girl never forgets when there's chocolate involved."

"Oh trust me, chocolate will be involved."

* * * *

The only logical explanation Tag could come up with was that Michaela's ex, Gary, was insane. Why on earth would a woman like Michaela be bad in bed? So much emotion in her tight little frame, he could only imagine she was a tiger in bed.

Tag splashed more cold water on his face when the simple thought made his jeans tight again. Her confession had set his brain back into first gear, but his libido was still in overdrive and he had to rein it in if he wanted to get anywhere with Kayla tonight. That's why he'd excused himself to go to the bathroom. The splashes of cold water weren't helping much, but they'd have to do. He couldn't leave her waiting any longer.

He took a deep breath and blew out to release the last of the frustration before he stepped out into the hall.

In the kitchen, Kayla leaned on the counter right by the

marshmallows. Bent until she almost laid flat on the counter eying the sweets, her hips swayed back and forth as she licked her lips.

"No cheating." His laughter was genuine when she jumped a few feet and clasped her hands behind her back. "Is the oil hot enough now?"

"Yes. I checked it just a few minutes ago. Can I see now, hmm?" She plucked a lollipop stick off the counter and held it out to him as he approached. "I'm dying here."

"You will be. These things are little bites of heaven." He grabbed the stick and set it down. "First the special surprise inside."

She turned and hopped up on the counter when he grabbed the chocolate. "I thought you were just drizzling that over top."

"That was the plan, and I still will. First." He stuck the tip of the bottle into the point of the marshmallow hard and gave one small, gentle squeeze. "Just a drop of chocolate inside for a surprise, and then I use the stick to fill the hole."

As he continued with several marshmallows in a row, she began to help, inserting the sticks as he finished with the chocolate. "I like it all ready."

"Then, the egg whites, and then coated well with the graham cracker crumbs. Making sure you cover it all. I think we can prep quite a few in advance the morning of so we aren't scrambling in the booth."

"Good idea." Once again she licked her lips, distracting him from his task for a moment.

He shook his head and turned to the oil. "Biggest deal will be to have someone just on marshmallow duty. They only take about ten seconds max, but it's best to move them around. And then…"

Her eyes widened when he pulled it out of the oil. "It kept its shape, and you've got the crumbs cooked perfectly. I'm impressed."

"Just wait." He grabbed the chocolate again and drizzled it over the marshmallow as he held it over a plate. "Now try."

Her tongue peeked out between her lips when she pulled it close. After just a moment to blow on it, she bit in. Bright blue eyes fluttered closed and her deep moan filled him with renewed need. She was determined to kill him. That was it.

"So," he said to cover his desire to yank her into a kiss. "You hate it, then?"

"Shhh." She held up her hand and it wasn't until the muscles of her neck twitched in her swallow that she said anything. "It's heaven on a stick."

The compliment warmed him further and he stepped closer. "So we'll use it for the Sweethearts On The Square Party?"

"Oh yeah." She stuck the rest of the treat in her mouth, but when she withdrew the stick, a string of marshmallow clung to her lip. Without finishing the second bite, she spoke around the marshmallow. "Definitely a keeper. That is so good."

He plucked the stick from her fingers and lifted his thumb to her lip. The way she stilled and her breath hitched drove him even closer. One strong swipe at the marshmallow only succeeded in smearing it across her lip. So he did the only logical thing, he leaned in to lick it off.

She offered up a delicate whimper when he sucked her

lip into his mouth, and her body jerked. As she arched toward him, he slid his arm around her waist and moved between her legs again. Her nails scratched across his scalp when she ran her fingers through his hair.

The sweet taste of marshmallow disappeared too quickly, so he tugged her closer until her head tilted back and her mouth opened for him. He swept his tongue through her mouth again, thrilled to hear her moan in response.

He released her waist long enough to yank the cord for the fryer out of the wall, never letting her free of the kiss. Every inch of her mouth was explored, and he pulled back to let her take her turn. The first hesitant touch of her tongue to his made his whole body hum, and he didn't bother to stop the moan. He braced one hand against the cupboard, and he let the other trail gently along her spine.

Once she'd explored for a moment, she gripped his hair and tugged him closer. Every effort went into not chuckling his pleasure, for fear she'd mistake it for teasing. Instead, he pressed his fingers into her lower back hard enough to press her delicious heat against his arousal. She unleashed another whimper that turned instantly into a moan.

Slowly he pulled back, licking his lips to savor her taste. He cupped her cheek, brushing his thumb along her delicate jaw line. "Kayla."

"Hmmm?" Hooded eyes, and a seductive lazy smile met his gaze. Damn, she was hot.

"Let me take you to your bedroom and prove you wrong."

There was a moment of hesitation and her hands fluttered down his chest, but she gave a small nod. "Yes."

* * * *

Click.

Michaela startled awake when the bedroom door shut. A light turned on down the hall and she furrowed her brow at the door in confusion. The moment she pushed to sitting, the night before came flooding back in a rush of delicious aches and erotic memories.

"Holy crap," she whispered. Had she really slept with none other than jail-bait himself, and had, what she could safely say was, her first orgasm ever? "Holy crap."

A grin split her mouth open as a shivering shudder ran through her at the memory of his touch. Without a doubt she wanted him again. Soon.

She bit her lip and flopped back onto the bed. *Shit.*

What if he was leaving, and not just getting something to eat? She heard him moving around in the kitchen, but he could just be cleaning up the mess they'd made.

With a groan, she curled on her side. *What if I was right? Oh God, how embarrassing.*

The clatter of several glasses followed by a curse from Owen stopped her depressing thoughts. What on earth was that boy doing? She sat up, half-tempted to go out and end her inner turmoil with a confrontation.

She chewed on her lip and drew her knees to her chest. Being paranoid was no way to end an incredible few hours. Although how Owen could be up at five in the morning when they'd been awake until at least two, she wasn't sure.

You're awake, you idiot. Yes, she was, but she always woke this early, and on this particular morning she could add in her panic. What was he doing?

For a moment she thought she heard the pop of a cork, but she had to have hallucinated it. Still, it didn't seem he was packing up to leave, after all he'd been in there five minutes. It wouldn't take that long to seal up the containers and run far and fast out of the apartment.

As long as he was gone, she might as well take care of personal business and brush her teeth. She scrunched her nose and ran her tongue over her teeth. A tooth-brushing was most definitely warranted.

She slipped out of bed and tugged her robe on, tiptoed into the bedroom's bathroom and shut the door. After she'd taken care of business and thoroughly brushed her teeth, she pulled out a spare toothbrush for him from the huge package her mother had bought her at the big-box store. Michaela had laughed at the necessity for one woman to have fifty toothbrushes at the time, but at the moment she was really grateful.

When she opened the door, she was surprised to see he still wasn't back. She frowned and walked to the bedroom door, ready to open it, but he was still moving around making noise. Curiosity might kill the cat, but she wasn't sure if it would be better knowing.

Maybe he was robbing her blind.

Shut up. Owen wasn't Gary. She had to stop being such an idiot.

A quiet rattling started to draw closer. Which meant he was probably coming back. She leapt back from the door and sprinted into the bed like a teenager caught sneaking around after curfew, she tossed off her robe and dove under the covers again.

She curled on her side, feeling like a complete fool. As

Owen crept into the room backwards, wearing nothing but boxer shorts and her apron, she couldn't stop her grin. He was adorably sexy, and she couldn't believe he was actually coming back into the room.

"You're up." He sounded almost disappointed. "I woke you when I knocked over the glasses, didn't I?"

"No." She rose with the sheet clutched to her chest. "I actually heard the door close. I'm an early riser; apparently no matter how late I get to sleep."

"Oh." There was a pout, but he wiped it away and shrugged. "Well, I brought some mimosas, and a couple Deep-Fried Sweethearts—and the chocolate. I did promise there would be chocolate."

This time she couldn't possibly mistake the desire in his eyes. Excitement stirred in her belly. "I guess you did. I—so last night…"

He sat on the other side of the bed and held out her glass. "Was amazing. You are amazing. Don't ever doubt that again. Then again, I like having to tell you just how sexy you are."

She felt a flush rising and drank a long swig of her mimosa.

"Drink up, I'm going to get cleaned up since you're awake…and then I'll get you dirty again."

She giggled and ducked her head. "I put out a toothbrush for you. Can I ask you to hurry?"

"I wish you would."

"Then hurry. Please." She down her drink and set it on the nightstand. The clock glared an angry 5:15 at her, the time she was usually working on paperwork or schedules or already making her way to the restaurant. She glared back and set her alarm for nine. The shop didn't open until noon, and she wanted to enjoy the rest of her morning if she could, and maybe catch a few more winks.

"Setting the alarm? You don't plan on sleeping do you?"

"I just don't want to be late." His suggestion that he wouldn't let her sleep thrilled her as much as the chocolate he brought into the room. She eyed him as he leaned on the bathroom doorframe. "You look good in my apron."

"I was frying sweethearts, and trying to avoid an oil burn."

"Still. I like the ruffles."

He darted toward her, and she squealed. Despite her attempt to duck away, he caught her and pinned her to the bed. His grin remained as he gave her a solid kiss. "I should keep the apron on then. After all, I'd hate to get chocolate on myself."

"Then what do you plan on doing with it?"

"Eating it."

"Okay."

"Off of you."

"Oh." She took a shaky breath. "So, why can't I do the same?"

"I knew there was a vixen in there."

* * * *

The only good thing about the busy evening they were having at The Midway was that Tag had to focus or he'd burn himself on the grill or with the fryer. As it was, he still couldn't keep from glancing up to watch Kayla on multiple occasions.

They'd spent each of the past three nights together, and Kayla had gone from repressed, nervous and timid to the tiger he'd expected. Better than that was her attitude around the shop. She smiled quicker, was relaxed more, and even took time to mill through the customers instead of hiding in her office when he was there.

If he wasn't careful his age-old crush could easily become an obsession.

"Howdy!" Clay waved from the other side of the counter. His wicked grin threatened continued teasing. From the moment Tag had stopped by to work on the car yesterday, Clay had known something was up, and had teased Tag thoroughly after congratulations.

Tag waved back and handed off the spatula to Cherie. As he approached Clay he held out his hand, but muttered, "Be nice. She's still shy."

"Wouldn't ever do anything to embarrass the lady." Clay chuckled. "Wanted to know if you'd be out at the shop tomorrow. If not I was gonna head out to the Neeley's ranch and go for a ride. Smokey is getting restless. The winter's been too long."

"Go on and get your ride in. I'm not working, but I have some errands to run for Aunt Myrtle. No worries. That hunk of metal isn't going anywhere." Tag laughed and clapped his shoulder. "Now what'll you have?"

"Just some caramel popcorn for the road. Shop's closed and it's movie night."

"Sure thing." Tag got Clay all set and out the door, and then quickly sought out Kayla.

He found her in the corner, in a close conversation with

Eve. The smiles she kept sneaking his direction let him guess the topic. At least she was telling someone outright. He was beginning to worry she was embarrassed to be with him.

With a shake of his shoulder he pushed away the moment of doubt and got back to work. Tables were wiped, drinks refilled, orders rang up, and eventually Kayla got back into the work end of things when she was done with her conversation.

When things settled and no new orders were coming in, she leaned on the edge of the counter. Even right then, in that small moment, she seemed more relaxed than he could recall her being. If he was the cocky sort he might crow about it—and he probably would when he got her home tonight.

"Good business tonight. I didn't expect us to be quite so busy. The movie playing next door isn't anything anyone wants to see." She absently wiped at the trays, chuckling low. "Then again, maybe that's why we were busy. They all came here instead of doing the movies first."

"Either way, it's a good night." He leaned on the counter next to her. "Have a good chat with Eve?"

"I did." She chewed her lip when he remained silent, then peeked at him through her lashes. "If you're asking, yes. I was talking about you. I hope that's all right."

"Of course it is. I told Clay." He kept his voice as low as hers, although the staff was mostly in the back cleaning up the grill and doing dishes while there was a lull.

"Oh my gosh." She pinched the bridge of her nose and took a deep breath. "Good to know. I'll try to rein in my embarrassment when I see him."

"What?" He frowned and leaned closer. "Kayla. Are

you ashamed of us?"

"What? Oh, no…not exactly. I mean…I just don't know what you told Clay is all. If it's anything like what you say to me."

"Locker room talk would never compare to the things I say to you."

Despite the flush creeping up her neck, she didn't stop the smile spreading across her features. "I suppose they are two totally different things."

"Besides. I wouldn't ever do anything to embarrass you. Remember, you're supposed to trust me." He leaned closer and tugged the towel from her hand. "You know, trust."

"I do—know. I'm trying."

"I know." He grinned and twirled the towel in his fingers. When she looked away to check the tables, he snapped it at her ass.

She shrieked and jumped, a mixture of shock, anger, and laughter crossing her features. Even though the whole restaurant had turned their direction, all of her focus was on him. "You little snot!"

He laughed and twirled the towel. "Come on. I promise I won't do it again."

"Don't you dare." She held up her hand and backed up until she hit the wall. Then a wicked grin spread across her lips and she spun, snatching a sopping wet towel out of the bucket and throwing it at him.

The sopping wet, and filthy, towel hit him smack in the chest, the end hooking over the top of his black apron. His jaw dropped as the cool water soaked right through his apron and shirt before the weight of the towel pulled it free and it hit the floor with a wet *plop.* "Ugh."

Her giggle drew his attention back to her, and the sopping wet towel she held in her hand. "Now you come on. I promise not to do it again."

Over the laugher in the room, a nasty voice called out. "Well, isn't this sweet?"

Every bit of joy sapped right out of Michaela and landed on the floor with the same wet *thud* the towel had when she dropped it. She tensed her jaw and drew up straight. "What do you want, Gary?"

"To see you, of course. Every time I try anywhere else, you shut me down. Although I didn't expect this." Gary scratched his chin through his goatee and wrinkled his nose in Tag's direction. "Stooped to cradle robbing, have we, Mikey?"

Tag couldn't help himself; he moved to take a protective stance by Kayla, but she shirked away. He frowned and narrowed his eyes at Gary. "Why don't you stop harassing her and get out of here or I'll call Sheriff Calvin."

"Oh sweet. He your guard dog now? Didn't you used to babysit him?" Gary chuckled. "I just can't believe it."

Kayla turned every shade of red until her entire face almost matched her hair. "Gary. Stop. You're just being an ass."

"Sleeping with a child—are you just getting off on being able to boss him around at work and in the bedroom?" Gary snorted. "Poor guy. Does he know you're not just supposed to lie there like you do?"

"That's enough." Tag grabbed his cell phone out of his pocket. "I'm calling Cal."

"This is a public place, you can't kick me out." Gary

sneered. "Child."

"Disturbing the peace ought to do it, I think." Tag scrolled through his contacts. Just when he opened up Cal's contact information, Gary scoffed and stormed toward the door.

As if it wasn't enough that he thoroughly embarrassed Kayla already, Gary paused as he drew open the door. "He'll realize there's better, Mikey. No one likes a dead fish in bed."

The bells above the door jingled into the silent restaurant as the door shut. Pale faces and wide eyes stayed diverted, focused on food rather than those at the counter. The utter emptiness of sound was erased when the door jingled open again.

As the new customer walked in, the rest returned to their meals, the spray of water behind him proved the employees were back to work. He reached toward Kayla's shoulder, but she jerked away and rushed back down the hall, slamming the office door.

While his first instinct was to rush to comfort her, he was torn as to what would be worse. If he went, he didn't care what the talk would say, but Kayla would. So, against his own desire, he stayed behind the counter working.

After another two hours the restaurant was down to just a few customers, none of which had been there when Gary had made his spectacular showing. Tag tugged off his apron and headed for the office.

She'd locked the door, but as he pulled out his keys he heard the *clunk* of the lock. He pushed it open, and stepped inside the dimly lit office. "Kayla."

"Don't." A small sniffle followed the forceful order.

"Just don't bother, all right?"

He moved toward the couch where she was curled up, but the second he got close she flew to her feet and tried to get around him. There was no way he was going to let her hide from this, or from the way she'd answered his question earlier.

Just before she got out of reach he grabbed her elbow and spun with her until she was pressed back against the door. She fought him for a minute. "Let me go."

"Are you embarrassed about us?"

"I…"

His heart sank and he released his hold on her elbow to brace both hands against the door.

Her chest rose and fell with rapid breaths that slowed and deepened. "Embarrassed is the wrong word. I'm not. I just…"

"Just what?"

"You may not care about our age difference, but they do. The talk that will go on. I've been talked about for years. A shotgun wedding, a cheating husband, a horrible divorce. I hate being talked about. I hate the whispers. We said we were taking this day-by-day. I barely know what I'm feeling, and I don't need to be judged while I figure it out."

"You're right. Embarrassed is the wrong word." His concern melted with her words, and more when her shoulders relaxed. "I get it, I think."

"You can't ever get it unless you've lived it. And you, golden boy, haven't."

He chuckled. "Golden boy? Really? You're going with that?"

"What would you prefer? Thor, God of Lake Point? Jail

Bait, the man all the women drool over as he passes?"

A groan rumbled through him and he placed his finger on her lips to quiet her. "Please stop. All I want to be thought of is the man that put that smile on your face, and makes you scream in bed. Or even, right here in this office."

"No."

"Oh yes."

"Owen."

"Yes?"

"Lock the door."

Chapter Five

Michaela's sexy hum topped of the husky note in her voice. "You are very convincing when you want to be."

Tag grinned and nuzzled her neck, not quite finished with her yet, though she tried to sneak down and snuggle. "All I did was suggest we take a break in the middle of the afternoon."

Two days ago he'd thought they were going to end up split apart, but here she was in his bed in the middle of the afternoon with only one week until the Sweethearts party. Her fingers trailed through his hair, weaving seductive little loops along his scalp. "It was more than a suggestion, and you know it. You molested me at my desk."

"Molested?"

She giggled. "Yes. I was innocently doing work—"

"Innocent. Pffft." He hopped up to his elbow and quirked a brow. "You had a frickin' lollipop."

"So?" Her brow furrowed, the innocent confusion once again made him doubt their age difference existed. "I had a craving."

"And it made me have a craving." His path back to her mouth was interrupted by a loud pounding on the door. The tension dropped out of his shoulders and he grumbled. "Damn it."

"Expecting someone?"

"No. It's probably crazy old Mrs. Quinn next door complaining about all the racket you were making in here. The screams of pleasure interrupted her reality TV with reality." The downfall of a duplex was shared bedroom walls. It hadn't been a problem until Michaela started coming over.

"Owen Frederick Montague!" She gasped and whacked him with a pillow. "You're horrible!"

"I'm honest." He snorted and ducked away from her next attack. Out of bed, he threw on his sweats and rushed out of the room with a pillow hot on his heels. Michaela had deadly aim, and he didn't plan on being the successful target.

The pounding resumed, and he groaned. "I'm coming, Mrs. Quinn. Sheesh."

When he opened the door, it definitely wasn't Mrs. Quinn. Gary sneered and tried to step into the house. "I know she's here, boy. Having fun screwing my wife?"

"Ex-wife. You can't come in here." Tag braced his arm against the doorframe. "Why don't you leave her alone? I think you've done enough to her."

"I've done?" Gary snorted. "She's the one that turned me in for drugs. Did she tell you that? Called Cal and turned me right in. She's a lying little bitch, don't believe everything she says."

"Everyone in town knows who the liar is." When Gary made a sudden move, Tag countered and tried to get him back out on the porch.

"Gary!" Michaela exclaimed behind him. Tag turned to find her clutching his robe around her, her features paling. "What are you doing here?"

In his surprise at her appearance, Tag lost his control of the situation, and Gary for a split second. Gary took full advantage and stormed into Tag's house, heading right for Michaela. She backed up several steps, but Gary managed to grab her elbow. "You're making a fool of yourself, Mikey."

"Let her go." Tag raced forward. Before he got all the way there, Gary spun and Tag saw stars as a sharp pain hit his nose. He grunted and gripped his nose, taking a full second to digest that Gary had punched him and Michaela was shouting something. Tag blinked a few times to clear his vision and moved fast to tackle Gary away from Michaela.

Gary flipped on him, and tried to scramble out from under. Tag managed to get to his feet just as fast. This time Tag got in a good punch, and Gary stumbled back. When Tag approached, the man stumbled back some more and bumped into the entertainment center.

Tag's brow furrowed, confused as to why the man had stumbled again, but shook it off quick to pay attention to the fight again when Gary took another swing at him. With a quick side step, Tag avoided the punch, but a sharp sting to his rib clued him into the second swing his adversary had made.

Gary's next attack came from behind and the tackle sent Tag toppling into his own entertainment center. The whole thing crashed down around them, and Michaela's garbled scream accompanied the shatter of glass and plastic and the crack of wood.

Tag growled against the disorienting pain in his nose, and the new aches and pains through his body. His left wrist was shot, but he had to get the upper hand. Tag might have been surprised by Gary's wily strength, but no longer.

The clatter of his DVD's and chunks of wood being tossed aside sounded on his right. Gary was on the move, and Tag flipped over onto his back. The moment Gary's face appeared, Tag kicked out with his leg and managed to just catch Gary in the side of the head.

Tag flew to his feet, the approaching sirens seeping into his awareness at the same moment he grabbed Gary's collar and dragged him toward the door.

Tires squealed in the driveway, a door slammed right after. Tag threw open the door and shoved Gary's stirring body onto the porch.

Sheriff Calvin stopped halfway up the porch steps. "Got calls from Mrs. Quinn several times today, and Michaela called while you two were fighting. What the hell happened?"

Before Tag could answer Mrs. Quinn started shouting from her porch, which was unfortunately attached to his. "I'll tell you what happened, and I'll thank you to watch your language, Sheriff."

"Mrs. Quinn," Cal spoke through clenched teeth.

Tag didn't have time to protest as Gary got to his feet then and started to advance again.

"First those two were making all sorts of loud and highly immoral sounds in the middle of the day, no less." Mrs. Quinn had her hoity-toity voice in full effect, but her words made Tag turn his back on Gary to check on Michaela. "I called you half an hour ago for them disturbing the peace, not that you came."

Gary took advantage of the disruption to try to wrestle past Tag. Once again disturbed from checking on Michaela, Tag tried to fight off Gary.

Cal glared in Gary's direction. "Mike, get Gary off this damn porch before I deck him. We need the situation calm, not his idea of a show. Now, Mrs. Quinn, what they were doing was not illegal."

"It is according to the bible." Mrs. Quinn scoffed, ignoring Gary's protest when one of the deputies stormed up the steps and pulled him away from Tag. "That little harlot was interrupting my shows with her screaming."

Michaela flinched and ducked further behind the doorframe, like she hoped the wood would swallow her whole. Once again her skin was bright pink, all the way down the V of flesh on her chest his robe left exposed.

"Mrs. Quinn!" Cal snapped. "I care about the fight. Tag, what happened?"

Tag wanted nothing more than to go to Michaela's side and take her in away from the prying eyes, but the moment he took a step her direction, she flinched back further. He frowned, but turned toward Cal. "Gary showed up here for no reason. Tried to grab Michaela, I stopped him. He blindsided me with a sucker punch to the nose."

"So I see. You're bleeding like a stuck pig. Here." Cal handed him a handkerchief. "Michaela, are you hurt?"

"N-no." Michaela clutched her hand to the neck of his robe, her eyes downcast. "Tag needs a doctor. His nose."

Tag's stomach twisted when she called him Tag instead of Owen. When he pulled the handkerchief from his nose, he shook his head. "I'm fine, Kayla."

A ghost of a smile flickered on her features before it was gone.

"Well, I never! Anyhow, as I was telling you, after they finally stopped banging on my wall and screaming, *he* showed up pounding on the door like he was trying to break in. I was terrified and called your people once again." Mrs. Quinn huffed and straightened her curls. "At least this time you listened."

"Thank you for your insight, Mrs. Quinn." Cal still gritted his teeth, and his smile looked more like he was in pain than anything. "Deputy Lawrence will take your statement. Tag, Michaela, why don't you go inside? I'll call in for trespassing and assault charges on Gary and be right in to get your statements."

Michaela didn't wait to be told twice, she disappeared into the house in a heartbeat. Tag nodded to Cal. "Thank you. We'll be inside."

Inside, Michaela paced back and forth, pausing at every turn to stare at the mess caused by the fight. She wrapped her arms around her waist when he drew close. A strained whisper broke the silence. "What the hell just happened?"

"Kayla. I'm sorry." Tag moved to hug her, but she shrank back.

"I need clothes. If he's coming back in, I should…"

Tag swallowed against the sudden lump in his throat when her departure was interrupted by the screen door creaking open. He sighed and shook his head as she started to clean up the mess instead. "What do you need for the statement, Cal?"

"I'll need to sit down with you both separately and get your statements is all. Shouldn't take but ten minutes. Is that all right, Mikey?" Cal tilted his head to look behind Tag. "Then you two can regroup and things can settle down."

"I guess." Michaela's voice was strained and could barely be heard over the clatter of DVD's. Then all sound stopped. When she spoke again torment and pain laced into every almost-wailed syllable. "Oh my God. No. Owen, no. Why?"

"Mikey?" Cal frowned and moved further into the room. "What's wrong?"

Tag cursed under his breath. All he wanted was five minutes to make sure Kayla was all right, and nothing was going how planned. He turned slowly to see what had caused her to react like that.

She stood with a shattered board from his entertainment center in one hand, in the other an old box he used to keep his handful of old computer CD's in. The top was missing and she stared into the box like it had a million spiders in it. "How could you?"

"How could I what?" Tag stepped toward her, but she turned a look of pure venom his direction. Never had a look made him back up a full step the way hers did. "Kayla, please."

Rather than answer, she held out the box to Cal. "Tell me it's not what I think it is, Cal. Please, tell me now."

Cal took the box, his brow furrowing as he reached inside. Plastic crinkled, and Cal leaned in for a moment. He pulled back suddenly and rubbed the end of his nose. "You know as well as I do it's what you think it is, Mikey."

She stepped closer to Cal and the two began a quiet exchange. With every whispered word, Michaela grew paler, tears streamed down her cheeks. One by one they dripped onto his robe, until she got still.

Tag opened his mouth several times to say anything, but couldn't seem to form a sentence. Something had happened, and Michaela's body language and distinct avoidance of his gaze confused the hell out of him.

Cal shook his head and this time his whispered words were just loud enough for Tag to hear. "Why don't you wait to hear what he has to say?"

Her hands curled up into fists at her side and a shudder ran through her entire body as she ripped her gaze from Tag's. "I can't be here. Can I do the statement later? Please."

"All right. How about I stop by when I'm done here? At your apartment?" Cal touched her shoulder in an oddly comforting gesture, even though Tag was the one dazed and confused.

"I'll be at The Midway. I have to work. I can't think about this, excuse me." Without another glance in his direction, she disappeared back down the hall. Her footsteps were silent, but the slam of his bedroom door wasn't.

There was no way she was just leaving, just like that. Tag's heart sank down to the floor. He took two steps toward the hall, but Cal stopped him. "What's going on?"

"Can you tell me how you ended up with marijuana in your desk, Tag?" Cal still held the box in his hand, a plastic bag clearly visible half wedged between two CD cases.

Confusion added to Tag's breaking heart and he shook his head. "I don't know what you're talking about. Gary was just in here, it's probably his."

"The top was on when Mikey picked up the box. It got knocked off by a piece of the cabinet she hit it on. This was already in here." Cal's voice was gentle, but Tag knew better than to think he wasn't digging for more.

"It's not mine." If he knew nothing else right then, it was that whatever that bag was, it wasn't his. He hadn't put it there, he'd never seen it before. When Michaela appeared and started through the room, he called out to her. "Kayla. You have to listen to me. It's not mine."

She stopped halfway across the room, her thick scarf hiding her features. "I've heard that before."

"You promised to give me the benefit of the doubt. Kayla, please listen." Instead of listening, she darted out the door and the screen closed with a bang. Tag clenched his jaw, and blinked against the sting of hurt threatening to bring tears about.

"I have to take you in, Tag. Trust me, I believe you, but I still have to take you in." Cal set a hand on his elbow. "Why don't you get dressed and we'll go down to the station. Call Myrtle so she can meet you down there."

Tag could only offer a nod, his whole body was numb. It moved on autopilot back to his room where he sank onto the edge of the bed and hung his shoulders. She'd turned her back on him, not waiting for an explanation, and not believing him one bit.

If only he'd listened when she said she was messed up. He wouldn't be there now, he wouldn't have been attacked by that no good bastard, none of this would have happened.

But then he'd never have gotten to see her in those elusive moments of joy and peace.

Damn her for turning her back on him. All he'd ever asked for was the benefit of the doubt. That's all. She couldn't even give him that.

He punched his fists into his knees and picked his head up to glare at his bloodied reflection. "Idiot. Idiot. Idiot."

With a ragged breath he rose and moved closer, narrowing his eyes at his counterpart on the other side of the glass. "The whole town tried to warn you, she tried to warn you, fucking Gary tried to warn you. Idiot."

His head dropped and he screwed his eyes shut. Damn it all to hell, it didn't matter. He'd started to fall in love with her anyway. Screw that, he already loved her, but he had to stop. Clearly she didn't love him back.

"Fool."

* * * *

Michaela chewed on what was left of her thumbnail, staring down the street on her right. She'd been at the stop sign for almost ten minutes. Thankfully the snowfall last night meant the roads were still quiet.

After almost a week of nearly turning down the street, she was still trying to build up the courage to do it. "Just turn the wheel and go."

A week ago she'd turned her back on Owen. She'd not given him the benefit of the doubt like he'd asked. Everybody in her life had read her the riot act for it, even Eve, although she'd done so more gently than the rest.

Still, she didn't know which part of her was the biggest fool. The one that had turned her back on Owen, even though life experience taught her that her judgment in men couldn't be trusted; or the part of her that wanted to believe in him more than anything.

"Just turn the wheel," she whispered. "There's a good chance he won't even open the door anyway, so just turn the wheel and go."

A car horn jolted her out of her inner struggle and she shrieked in surprise. With an apologetic and embarrassed wave out her back window, she turned down Owen's street.

The other car went the other direction, so she was able to drive slowly down the street. Still she arrived at his duplex all too soon and parked her car across the street.

At this point she didn't know where to begin, or even what she was feeling or thinking any longer. Ever since his abrupt, and very justified, resignation, she'd been at a total loss. When he'd come into The Midway to turn in his keys she'd found herself unable to even speak.

Even though he was only out on bail, she'd doubted her own initial reaction to finding the pot immediately, maybe he wasn't guilty. Familiar doubts interrupted every one of her own attempts to believe his innocence.

She should've said she was sorry. Thrown herself at his feet and begged forgiveness.

But the familiar doubt, the safe wall of seclusion she'd built so long ago, had crept back up and prevented it. What if the drugs had been his?

How could she believe that about him?

She'd never thought it was possible with Gary either.

Already she knew the charges had been dropped, although she didn't know why. The rumor mill of Lake Point moved faster than blizzard winds some days, but it didn't always carry every detail. No matter what the reason, he'd been cleared of the charges.

He was innocent according to Cal. That's all that should matter.

No, what should matter is believing in her heart that he was innocent.

She knew she did, even if she doubted her own ability to pick a good man. Her initial reaction to finding the drugs was instinct, after her past it should be expected.

Unfortunately, Owen didn't know any of that. Would he listen to her story now? Did she deserve that?

Maybe Owen would hear her out if she started with sorry. First step would be finding her voice, and not locking up like she had when he'd come in to quit.

Before she could quadruple guess herself yet again, she grabbed her keys and got out of the car. She trucked across the street and up the steps despite her nagging doubts and the nosy Mrs. Quinn's curtains moving aside to stare at her. With more force than she thought her trembling hands capable of, she pushed the doorbell.

Silence echoed back and she tapped her heels rapidly on the porch. "Please, Owen. Please, answer the door. Please, please, please."

She chewed on her lip and glared toward Mrs. Quinn's not-so-subtle peeping face. With a deep frown, she hit the doorbell again.

The door cracked open finally, but it wasn't Owen on the other side. Myrtle herself fixed a scolding scowl on Michaela. It was enough to stop Michaela's tapping heels, and lodge the thick lump of fear firmly in her gullet.

"Please." Michaela cleared her throat when the word squeaked at an embarrassing pitch. She twisted her fingers together and bit her lip. "Can I see him?"

"Look, Missy." Despite her lack of coat, Myrtle stepped onto the porch and pulled the door shut securely behind her. She urged Michaela toward the railing across from the door. "I know your reasons for what you did, and that you got your demons."

"He needs to know them, and I need to apologize." Michaela twitched her nose against the tingling rise of renewed tears she'd thought were long dry. "I know."

"Nobody knows your story but you. I know there's been a heap of talk around these parts, but talk is just that." Myrtle frowned. "But if you hurt my boy again…"

"I doubt he'll even take me back. I just want to tell him…"

"Oh, sugar. You and he, you're in for a mess of trouble if you keep up with all this denial." Myrtle sighed, and patted Michaela's hand. "He's good and hurt, and he's got every right to be. But I told him to try to talk to you. Was trying to get him to go today. I can't guarantee he'll talk to you, but you can try."

"Thank you." Michaela followed Myrtle to the door, and stepped into the warm house right behind the older woman. In the kitchen, Tag rose to his feet and scowled between Myrtle and Michaela.

"Tag, don't give me that look. I got to get my old body into work and I don't have any more time for your stubborn head. Now give me a kiss and then at least listen for five minutes." Myrtle shrugged on her enormous coat and leaned her cheek to Tag.

Tag kept a dark eye on Michaela, but leaned sideways and placed a half-assed kiss on his aunt's cheek. As the woman ambled toward the back door and disappeared outside, he remained immobile and silent.

Once again Michaela could swear she felt every single word in her head tumble over each other until they curled into a snarled ball and shot right down into a lead ball in her gut. Doubt over the right course of action started to creep back up.

"Well? You're down to four minutes."

His voice startled her right out of her own misery and she met his hard gaze with wide eyes. Her mouth opened and closed impotently for what had to be another minute before she managed to find her voice. "I'm sorry."

"Thanks. Doesn't take my night in jail away, or erase my name out of the paper under arrests—"

"I hurt you. I embarrassed you. I can't ever make it right and I don't expect you to ever forgive me. I should have said something when you came to the shop, but I didn't know what to say, or how I felt, I was so confused."

"That makes two of us." He turned his back on her and leaned on the counter. His shoulders twitched and he picked at the loose edge of the marbled laminate. "I only ever asked you for one thing—to give me the benefit of the doubt. You couldn't do that, could you?"

"I told you I couldn't. I told you I could only try. With my track record, I wasn't sure what to think. You can't begin to understand."

"You wouldn't even let me try. All that time I thought you were starting to open up, you weren't. I was lying to myself."

"No, you weren't. It's not your fault."

"I'm a fool for thinking I could crack that shell."

"No. You cracked it, but a crack takes time to widen. Time we didn't have." She closed her eyes and dropped her head. "Will you let me explain why—why I walked away, why I still struggle to believe you are a good guy even though I know—I *know* that I should?"

"So you still don't believe I'm innocent? Then why are you here?"

"Because in my experience good guys just don't exist!"

Michaela had a flash of anger and embarrassment so strong she had to shrug off her coat to try to erase the prickly heat. "I told you I was messed up. Do you want to know how? Is that what you wanted to know all along?"

"Yes!"

"Fine. My first boyfriend took my virginity—but he didn't stop there. He took my money, my jewelry and then stole from the grocery store, a few of his neighbors cars, and then stole a computer from the school and ended up in juvie." She glared out the window at the snow. "My second boyfriend seemed like such a great guy until he tried to date rape me, saying he knew I was easy thanks to boyfriend number one."

Tag didn't speak, but one fist slowly lifted from the counter and pressed back down like a slow motion punch.

"Boyfriend three managed to pass my six months dating rule and get me in bed, only to point out that he'd been sleeping with some freshman so he wouldn't push me when I clearly wasn't ready. As he put it, he was just soothing his urges so we could get to know each other."

"After that I gave up for a while. Finished out high school alone, and went to college at SUNY." Michaela snatched her coat from the floor and gathered it against her chest. "Then there was Gary who, believe it or not, was once just like you."

Tag snorted and shook his head. "Please."

"Really. Ask Myrtle. She'll tell you. We were both in school for science. I eventually moved into business, and he, well he gave up on school because his family couldn't afford it any longer. He was cute, funny, sweet, smart; a real catch. For once I thought my instincts might be on course. Maybe it was my fault in the end, I don't know." She sank into the closest chair. "I didn't handle what happened with the pregnancy well, after all."

The slow motion punch ended and his back drew up straight. "What happened? I know the rumors, but I don't know everything."

She exhaled slowly. "That's a whole heap of another mess, that I'd be happy to tell you when we aren't talking about my screwed up choice in men…if you still want to hear it."

On stiff legs he walked to the chair on the opposite end of the table and sat.

"Short of it is, the rumors of the shotgun wedding are relatively accurate. I took a pregnancy test, it was positive. He did the supposed right thing and asked, my parents paid for us to fly to Vegas and get hitched." She tucked a loose lock of hair back up in her hat. "I don't know if he was already doing drugs at that time, I guess it was possible. I was pretty clueless then. Oblivious, actually."

"How so?"

"Oh, I had friends that used. Somehow, I just never knew. It wasn't until we were out camping one weekend and someone mentioned that they were smoking it that I realized what was going on. I was oblivious and didn't ever want to even experiment. I guess my friends knew I had no interest and so they'd never offered."

"Or you didn't want to know, so you ignored it was there."

"Maybe." She picked at the zipper on her coat, taking a deep breath. "I suppose Gary might have been taking part with them then, I wouldn't know. I never asked, and he never told. We got married, started planning for the baby, which my parents were all too happy to help with. Then I went to the doctor and learned the pregnancy test had been a false positive there was no baby, just a huge mess of trouble."

He sprang forward when her tears started, but then seemed to realize what he'd done and sank back into his chair.

She sniffed and swiped a tear from her cheek, clearing her throat again. "Anyway, it sent me into a depression. I guess Gary took that as a signal that he didn't have to be the good guy any longer. You know, he slept with a hooker on our wedding night. After all, when you're in Vegas you have to sleep with a hooker. He told me that as he signed the divorce papers."

On the table his hands clenched so tight his knuckles turned white.

"I don't even know if the downfall was fast or slow. I was in such a horrible place and Gary couldn't see fit to support me in my pain. He told me to get over it and get a job or something." She chewed on the insides of her cheeks as she tried to reconcile the inner conflict. "It was three years into our marriage when I started to wake up. When I found the first stash of drugs in a shoe in his closet."

She shrugged. "I wanted to believe he was the guy I dated in college. I didn't know the guy I dated in college was dating other women. Like I said—oblivious. So I confronted him. We fought, we talked, he agreed to marriage counseling. I thought we might finally get our lives back together, but we didn't. Well, I was trying, he was still being Gary."

"So why didn't you leave?"

After a bitter laugh, she nodded. "Once I found more drugs, and then sex tapes, six months after we were supposed to be working on things, I did. It just took another year and a half to finally come to an end. I spent another two years trying to piece myself together after that mess was over, Owen. The Midway got me out of that hole. But you…"

He flinched and turned his gaze away.

"You're what brought me back to life. I was skeptical of my own happiness because of my past. I've lived the lie of 'too good to be true', so when I found that stash, I was sure I was living it again. I don't want to live it again."

"It wasn't mine. If you can't believe me at my word, then there's nothing left for us."

"I know."

He took a ragged breath. "Your track record sucks. I guess I can understand why you reacted like you did—but you have to leave now if you still have doubts."

With a shaky breath, she rose to her feet. As she stared at the collar of the coat in her hands, she shook her head. "It's not you I doubt. It's myself. You are a good guy. I know in my heart you are, and I need to believe you."

Silence echoed through the tiny kitchen, he offered her no reprieve, not that she deserved one.

She shook her head and slipped her coat on. "You deserve better than me. You're young, you have a long life in front of you. It doesn't matter any longer if I believe in your innocence, I already hurt you, embarrassed you, and I don't know if I can be fixed. You deserve better."

"I probably do."

Her heart sank and she forced a smile that only lasted a moment. "I know you do."

"I still want to know. Do you believe the drugs weren't mine?"

Chapter Six

The silence became almost unbearable. Tag could practically see the internal struggle Kayla fought to answer his question. She'd said her doubt was with herself, and whether he deserved her, but the lingering silence made him start to question if it was her doubts about him.

"I believe you," she whispered so quiet he could hardly hear her over his own pounding heart. "I have hated myself since I walked out of this house, every minute of every day since I did. I was just so ashamed for turning my back on you, and every time someone chastised me for what I'd done, it just added fuel to that fire. Plus, I've known all along I don't deserve your forgiveness."

Every bit of that last week's stress blew out in one long breath. Her departure had cut him deep, but it was her continued absence that had killed him. He'd thought when he went to turn in his keys she might stop him, or say something, but she'd kept silent. "When I stopped by to quit?"

"I locked up. You didn't say a word. This was beyond simple embarrassment for me; it was shame. I couldn't bring myself to say anything, even apologize, which I knew I needed to. It's taken me a week to build up the courage to drive down this street." She tugged her scarf tight around her neck and tucked it into her coat. "I'm sorry. Truly, deeply sorry. I hope you have a happy life. You deserve it."

"Wait." Even through his lingering pain he couldn't let her walk away again. God, he'd fallen in love with her, and though she'd hurt him, he hadn't stopped. "Cal sent the stash to some lab to check for fingerprints. He knew it wasn't mine."

"They were Gary's." She turned to face him again, her face streaked with tears. "Right?"

"Yeah."

"He doesn't want me happy." Well, she was putting it lightly. "Brenda told me he stopped in when we were at the hockey game. Said he disappeared for a while. I didn't think anything of it at first, but I had Cal check and someone jimmied the lock on the office. I don't know what he was after in there, but the more I thought about it, the more I realized he's good at picking locks. If he got into my office, he could have easily gotten into your house."

"You were happy."

"I was."

He rose and took a step toward her. Her breath hitched and she ducked her head. After a deep breath, he shook his head. "You did hurt me."

"I know."

"I have another confession."

A small whimper sounded into the room, and she shook her head.

"Before you walked out that door, I was falling in love with you." With another step he cut the distance between them in half. She tried to back up, but hit the frame of the narrow door. "Hurt as I've been, I haven't been able to stop loving you. That's why it hurt so much when you left. That's why I kept forgiving you every time the hurt came back. I wanted so bad to be angry, I tried, and I was, but always—"

"Wait. Please. Let me confess my secret before you say anything further, anything you might regret." Her hand planted on his chest when he tried to close the distance. "You are so young."

"Stop saying that."

"I can't have children, Owen. If you ever hope to be a father the natural way it would never be with me. There is no future here, and I won't let you waste time here on me."

He froze, one hand braced on the counter, the other half lifted toward her down-turned face. No children. When she'd talked about the false positive pregnancy tests, she'd said 'a whole mess of trouble.' Apparently she wasn't kidding.

"I know marriage, kids, all of that isn't something even on the table, but before you think of forgiving me, before you think of telling me you love me, you have to know that. It's only fair and I should have told you sooner, but I hate talking about it. No one knows."

The shock subsided enough that he resumed his hands course toward her chin and tugged her gaze up to his. "The false positive?"

"It was a mass. Benign, but large. Their best guess is it started on an ovary, and just took over. It consumed my ovary and half of my uterus before I got the needed ultrasound." Fresh tears spilling her old and deep pain trickled along her cheekbone and into her hair. "That's what sent me into the depression."

"What he told you to get over."

"They were able to save an ovary so I wouldn't go into

menopause. What was the big deal?" Bitterness laced her words and wrinkled her nose. "So please, let me go so you can live a life full of hope and less mess than I can offer you."

"I don't think I can." He cupped her cheeks in his hand. "Maybe I should, but I don't want to walk away."

"But your future."

"Is mine to choose."

"I'm broken."

"Well I have an arrest record now."

"An arrest record that's my fault."

"No." He shook his head and held her gaze. "It was Gary's fault. What happened with us, it was our fault. I guess we both messed up."

"Can you ever forgive me?"

"I have over and over again already. Can you learn to trust me?"

She set her hands on his and met his gaze. "It's trusting myself that I struggle with. I told you, I suck at this."

"You also told me you were bad in bed." The familiar red hues of her sexy blush bolstered his mood even further. "And you were very wrong about that, too."

"But I proved myself right here. I turned my back on you."

"In a way I did the same." He sighed and dropped his hands. They had to change the subject before they wallowed in their own misery. "I want to move past this and start again, but…"

When his voice trailed off she froze, tears still dancing on her lashes. "But?"

"Considering how you feel about criminals, can you

ever be with a man that has been to jail, even for a few hours? It changed me…I'm a hardened criminal. A badass."

"How much was in the bag?" She quirked a brow, the shimmer of tears fading. The change of tone to teasing appeared to have the right affect.

"Cal said it was about sixteen and a half ounces." He smirked. "Why?"

"It's only a class D felony, then. Tell me when you've been arrested for possessing over ten pounds. It's not until you get to class C felonies that you can call yourself a badass. Besides, the drugs weren't yours, so where's the cool factor in that?"

"Michaela O'Keefe, are you teasing me?"

"Maybe."

He grinned and plucked the hat off her head. "I think we need a new set of rules if we are going to do this. I want to trust you, and I want you to trust me."

"I want the same, but—"

"No. No buts." He brushed a lingering tear from her cheekbone. "The reports say there's a storm coming into town tonight. Close the shop today. We are going to talk for as long as it takes until we are both sure about this."

"I've never closed the shop. Even during the blizzard last year."

"You didn't have anything else then. This time you do."

A tremulous smile started to form and she nodded. "All right. Just for tonight."

"Just for tonight. Go call the staff. I'll get a few things together. We'll go to your place."

"Mine?"

"It's closer to the shop, and you don't have a change of

clothes here, do you? I'm not letting you leave in the middle of a snowstorm because you don't have clean panties."

She blushed and shook her head. "Will you ever stop teasing me?"

"Afraid not."

"Good." Her smile warmed up his heart and took an eraser to the lingering concerns and fears he struggled to let go of.

Before he left the room he snaked an arm around her waist and pulled her close. When he leaned in for a kiss, this time she wasn't the only tentative one. Her tender response and the soft touch of her hand to his cheek eased more of his worry. When he pulled back he let out a shaky breath. "I want this to work."

"I'm worried too. I don't want to hurt you again, and I'm so good at messing things up."

"You didn't mess up the shop."

"The shop isn't a human being. You are."

"Answer me one question."

She looked at him through her lashes and nodded. "I'll try."

"How do you feel about me?" After his earlier confession, she hadn't responded in kind. While he knew it could take time, and that she'd had to confess, he wanted to know going in where she was.

The lingering blush on her cheeks deepened to a dark rouge, but she didn't hide away this time. Instead, she took a shuddering breath and set her hands on his biceps. "I've had all week to think about this. I thought it was just a crush, but it wasn't. I care about you—you brought me back to life and yes…"

Tag held his breath, tugging her closer.

"I think I was, am, falling in love with you. Love scares the crap out of me."

"I know."

* * * *

The Sweethearts On The Square Party went on as planned despite the snow. The planning team had prepared for a snow event. After all, it was February, and the large tent that spanned the entire side-block of the square had strategically placed heaters for those gathered inside.

The Midway's station was set up right in front of the restaurant itself so Michaela, Owen, or any of the staff could sneak back inside for supplies. Outside the tent, around the courthouse grounds, and through the adjoining street were snow games and events, and someone had put the ice rink back up from the tree lighting back in November.

Strong arms circled Michaela's waist, and a warm teasing kiss was placed on her neck. The tickling scratch of Owen's new stubble sent a jolt of excitement down her spine right to her core. He pressed his lips to her ear lobe and spoke low. "Every single one of them looking our way is gossiping, judging."

The familiar stirring of unease threatened to ruin her mood, but she just nodded. "I know. Three days ago we weren't talking, after all."

"Not just that. They searched Gary's car, found more than that weed he snuck into my place. Cal says the prosecutor's talking a minimum of fifteen years with all they found in his car. Including some things of yours."

Michaela stopped rearranging the cupcakes and straightened. "What?"

"Brenda, will you cover the table for a few minutes?" Owen waved her over and tugged Michaela's hand. He pulled her into the shop where Cal held a box in his hands.

"Afternoon, Michaela. Sorry to interrupt the party. Everything was processed and Sharon gave me clearance this morning to return your things to you." Cal set the box on the table. "Sharon guesses he was trying to find a way to leech your business accounts. It's financial records, your business plan, and some jewelry."

Things she hadn't even noticed were missing. "I had them locked in my hidden file in the desk. I didn't even think to look when I realized my office had been broken into. I didn't think he'd find them, much less break the lock."

"Turns out he's got warrants out in a few states. Pretty sure we'll get him locked away for a long time this time, Mikey." Cal set a hand on her shoulder. "I'll let you get them put away and get back to your party. Sharon said to call her any time and she'll schedule an appointment to fill you in on what you need to know."

"Thank you, Cal." Michaela smiled as best she could and set her hands on the box. "If you talk to her again today, tell her I'll call her on Monday."

"Will do." Cal touched the tip of his hat and shook Owen's hand before heading to the door.

The moment the door jingled shut, she ripped the top off the box. "The bastard."

Owen pulled out a few file folders, then withdrew a ring box. "Wedding ring?"

"I was going to happily pawn it to start the business, but

Mom and Dad told me to hold onto it for when I felt I could splurge on something, not for a need, but a want. I haven't had any sort of chance to use it yet. Shit, he took mom's bracelet."

He let out a low whistle when she withdrew the glittering tennis bracelet. "Wow."

"Mom's best piece. I used it for a cousin's wedding and haven't had a chance to return it yet. That's what sucks about them being down in Virginia." She sighed and dropped it into the box. "He pretty much wiped out my private safe. I can't believe I didn't look sooner."

"He's gone now. Will be for a long time." Owen set his hand on hers. "Let's put this away in the safe. We'll get the combination and keys changed soon as possible so you can feel safe again. Then, we'll get back to the party. We've got some Deep-Fried Sweethearts to sell."

"They're selling really well. You are a genius, Owen. Don't ever quit."

"The Midway—or you?"

"Both."

Epilogue

One Year Later

All of the trappings and trimmings of Sweethearts On The Square were gone. Owen's latest genius candy, The Captured Heart, had been even more popular than the Deep-Fried Sweethearts. Business was going better than ever, and Michaela had promoted Owen to full manager and hired two new assistant managers.

Gary's trial, after being dragged out by postponements, had landed him in prison for a good long time. For some reason the bastard still wrote her, but she threw out his letters without ever reading them. Life was too good to linger in the past any longer.

Of all the good things in her life, Owen was by far the best. True to his promise, she'd come to relax and learn to trust not only him, but herself again. Moments of doubt still crept in, but she was learning to cope with them.

When his lease was up he'd left the duplex next to nasty Mrs. Quinn and moved into the open apartment above hers. She had to admit, she appreciated that he was right there all the time, but she still had her own space and he had his. Maybe in the future they'd change the arrangement, but right then it was perfect.

"You ready?" Owen leaned on the doorframe and quirked that crooked smile she loved so much. "Or are you going to fight me on this as much as you fought me on loving me."

"I didn't fight you. I've loved you for a long time, I just fought admitting it."

"Oh, I see." He chuckled and approached the desk in her now significantly smaller office. In order to accommodate the new managers, she'd had to move the wall and cut back on her over a dozen file cabinets so she could keep the couch she and Owen enjoyed so much. "Put the papers away. There's nothing left to handle here. Everything that needs to be done in the next two weeks is next door in the assistant manager's office."

She rose and nodded. "I know. I still can't believe I'm doing this."

"What? Spending a whole two weeks with me?"

"No. Leaving The Midway in someone else's hands that aren't yours, for two whole weeks." Once the new managers had been hired it had been her choice, not his. She'd pawned her wedding ring and planned a cruise with Owen. Her mom and dad were coming up to watch the restaurant for her, and she was actually going on vacation.

"It was your idea."

"I know. I think it might be the best idea I've had since The Midway." She grabbed her bag off the floor and stepped into his waiting arms. "Too bad we can't bring Lucy and Betty with us."

He chuckled at her mention of their cars. Over the past year she'd helped him restore Lucy, and she was almost perfect, they were just waiting on a few parts and the paint. All of which would come in while they were in the Caribbean. "Lucy's not ready for a play date, and the weather is horrendous. I'm not subjecting my baby to these salted mess of roads."

"Good boy." She grinned. "Maybe this summer we'll sneak down to Virginia with her and get those two beautiful girls together."

"Planning another vacation all ready? Damn, I'm impressed."

"What can I say? You're a terrible influence on me." She grinned when he leaned in close. "A terrible influence I rather thoroughly enjoy having in my life."

"The feeling is mutual." He brushed his lips across hers and tugged her closer. "What time is our flight?"

"We don't have time for a quickie. We have to leave for the airport five minutes ago."

He groaned, but nodded. "Fine. Maybe at the airport."

"Owen," she warned, but his only reply was to pinch her ass. She laughed and swatted at his hand. "Stop it. We have to go. We'll have plenty of time for quickies and long, slow, luxurious sessions on the cruise."

"You are a wicked little vixen."

"I didn't used to be. It's all your fault."

"And it's something I'll never, ever regret." He chuckled and took her bag, slinging it over his shoulder. "Let's go. I hear ocean breezes calling my name."

"And warm sun to burn my pasty skin."

"I packed lots of sunscreen." He pursed his lips as they walked through the quiet restaurant and out the front door. "I want to be able to touch every inch of you all the time, no sunburns allowed."

She chuckled and tugged the door closed, locking it with a sigh. "There. It's done. I'm on vacation."

"I promise, you won't regret it."

"Oh, I don't doubt you. Two weeks with the ocean, the beaches, and the man that I love? I can't see anything I regret in that mix."

"Say that again." He held the door half open and grinned.

"What? The ocean?"

"Nope."

"The beaches?"

"Nuh-uh." He leaned closer and brushed his cold nose with hers. "Try again."

"The man that I love. It's not the first time I've said it."

"I know. I just never tire of hearing it."

The End

Up Next in Lake Point
Stalled Independence

Chapter One

"No, not here." Amanda whined. The car sputtered and spurted. It barely made it to the shoulder before dying. She hit the steering wheel hard, like that would do her any good, and dropped her forehead to the wheel.

Tears she'd managed to keep at bay since Pennsylvania welled up again. She had no idea where she was, other than New York. She'd gone through Rochester in hopes of seeing Lake Ontario, but hadn't been able to find her way back to the I-90. She'd taken the first highway she could find headed east, but had no idea if it would take her back to the 90, or where she'd end up. Her last thought would be that her car would choose here of all places to die.

She lifted her head, wiping the tears from her eyes so she could see. The road sign ahead read 'Lake Point. 1 mile'. A groan escaped and she dropped her head to the steering wheel. A solid thump resonated through her already pounding head, taking the decibel level of her headache to near migraine levels. "What am I going to do?"

There was nowhere left to go. She'd had no destination in mind, and should've been grateful the car had taken her this far from Illinois.

A shuddering breath racked her lungs and a sob tore from her gut. For three days she'd driven all over the place. She didn't want to follow a straight line, and half the time had felt lost.

Who was she kidding, all she felt was lost. Her location no longer mattered.

A sharp knock on the window startled a shriek out of her.

"Ma'am? Y'all right in there? Do you need a hand?" Another tap on her window drew her toward the window and the—the fricking cowboy standing outside.

A cowboy? Her hands shook too hard to move, and she imagined she looked frightful. The way his eyes widened didn't lessen that belief. She pressed down her lock and nodded. "I'm fine. Go away. I'll call someone."

"Sorry I startled you, miss." A smile broke on the disturbingly handsome face. "Name's Clay. It's right smart of you not to open up. You got someone to call?"

No she didn't. Worse, the pay-as-you-go phone she'd bought was dead after her last call to Grace. At this point in time she had no one to call. No one but the man outside her window, but she wasn't about to get out and hitch a ride with a perfect stranger.

"How about I call Sheriff Calvin? And I'll call for a tow and have the car taken to my garage." Clay apparently took her silence for an acknowledgement that she didn't know what to do. He turned on his phone and started calling.

All she could do was nod rapidly, even after he'd turned

away. She had no idea what else would work. Her voice didn't want to function, the world had crashed in when the car died. The reality of what she'd done, and how alone she was, dug at the dark hole in her soul until her lip trembled again.

Thankfully the cowboy backed off and went back to his truck. It left her free to try to gather herself together. She turned the rear view mirror toward herself and let out a bitter laugh. Red splotched her face, the damn dark circles under her eyes a deep purple now that the makeup had been cried and wiped away.

She sniffled and wiped at her cheeks to remove the last salty vestiges of the 'hysterical woman' she'd so often been accused of being. At this point maybe she should have felt relief, but she felt more scared than ever.

Five minutes later flashing lights came into view at the edge of her mirror and she shifted it back to get a better view. A cop car had pulled up behind Clay and the sheriff now stood shaking the man's hand. So he wasn't a homicidal maniac, or if he was he was a damn good one.

A strangled laugh choked out and she cleared her throat. After a long exhale and a shake to remove the last of her nerves, she unlocked the door again. By the time the cop got to her car she felt somewhat composed, even if she looked like hell.

"Everything all right, miss?" The short man stood at the ready, one hand on his holster just in case she was the homicidal maniac. Not that she blamed him after the show she'd just put on. No wonder Tony always said she was too emotional.

The mere thought brought up a whimper so fast she

couldn't stop it. Luckily it wasn't a full on sob, and she was able to nod. "My car broke down. I've got no one to call. I'm just…"

"It's okay. Clay's already called a tow for you. If anyone can fix this, he can." The man reeked of doubt when he took in the car. It was a heap of junk, and she knew it. "How about I give you a ride to the garage? You can wait for it there."

There wasn't anything else to do. Short of finding another heap of junk that would wipe her out of the last bit of money she had. If there was a higher power, it was telling her to stop where she was. With a long sigh she shrugged. "I suppose. So he's okay?"

Sheriff Calvin glanced back to the truck and snorted. "Clay? He's harmless. Don't bite or nothing. Damn good with cars, too. Don't let the cowboy thing freak you out. We try not to."

She allowed an uneasy laugh and grabbed her purse. Once she stepped out, she took a deep breath. "Thank you."

"No problem. I'm Sheriff Calvin, most people just call me Calvin. And this here is Clay Ryley." Calvin gestured to the cowboy.

Clay tipped his hat. "Sorry again about startling you, Miss. I saw you stall out and thought I'd try to help."

"I appreciate it. Sorry for, well, this." She gestured to her face. "It's been a long drive."

"No problem. You go on with Cal, I'll wait for the truck."

She nodded and let the sheriff lead her toward his car. Before she got in, she chanced another glance at the cowboy. Figures on the one day in her life she met a hot cowboy she was a total wreck. Death warmed over probably looked better.

With a sigh, she slid into the car and pulled her purse tight against her chest.

The End

About the Author

Sarah Cass' world is regularly turned upside down by her three special needs kids and loving mate, so she breaks genre barriers; dabbling in horror, straight fiction and urban fantasy. She loves historicals and romance, and characters who are real and flawed, so she writes to understand what makes her fictional people tick. And she lives for a happy ending – eventually. And enough twists to make it look like she enjoys her title of Queen of Trauma Drama a little too much.

An ADD tendency leaves her with a variety of interests that include singing, dancing, crafting, cooking, and being a photographer. She fights through the struggles of the day, knowing the battles are her crucible; she may emerge scarred, but always stronger. The rhythms to her activities drive her words forward, pushing her through the labyrinths of the heart and the nightmares of the mind, driving her to find resolutions to her characters' problems.

While busy creating worlds and characters as real to her as her own family, she leads an active online life with her blog, Redefining Perfect, which gives a real and sometimes raw glimpse into her life and art. You can most often find her popping out her 140 characters in Twitter speak, and on Facebook.

Sarah Cass

Books by Sarah Cass

The Tribe Series
The Tribe
The Wolf
The Chief
The Raven
The Dominion Falls Series
Changing Tracks
Derailed
Dark Territory
Runaway Train
Home Signal
The Lake Point Series
Santa, Maybe
Deep-Fried Sweethearts
Stalled Independence
Witch Way
A Thorough Thanksgiving
Eve's New Year
Heartstrings & Hockey Pucks
Luck of the Cowgirl
Stars, Stripes & Motorbikes
Free Falling
Love for Hire
Stand Alone Novels
Masked Hearts
Leap

Divine Roses Ink